Amber Aitken

The CUPID Company

Forever and Ever

HarperCollins *Children's Books*

Forever Friends

The ocean tide was at its lowest, the boats sitting high and dry on the yellow beach sand. Early-morning fishermen stood chewing sandwiches while they fished. Somewhere up above in the salty air, white seagulls circled and squawked for their breakfast. The promenade and beach were otherwise deserted, but Coral and her pup Romeo barely noticed. They were running far too fast.

On the other side of the Sunday Harbour seafront, Nicks was also racing along. Pretty beach houses of sea blue and green stood quietly as she passed them by. Shops were empty too. Not that Nicks noticed.

Coral and Romeo sped past the cobbled jetty and a huddle of beached buoys, with the wind whistling in their ears like a hurricane.

Nicks's heart beat so fast it made her chest burn. But that didn't slow her down one bit. She swiped at the tears streaming down her cold cheeks and ran even faster.

Coral was the first to spy Coral Hut as it stood quietly in line with the rest of the sleeping beach huts. The sight of its pale pink, minty-green and lemon-yellow stripes spurred her on, and she put all her energy into her final sprint.

Finally Nicks reached the promenade. There was Coral Hut! She dipped her head and moved her arms even faster.

The two girls arrived at their beach hut at

precisely the same time. But then they were best friends; they did almost everything together.

"Coral!"

"Nicks!"

"I got here as quickly as I could," cried Coral breathlessly. "I left the moment you called. Are you all right?"

Nicks was also trying to catch her breath. She was sobbing at the same time, which made catching her breath just about impossible. And talking was out of the question. Coral immediately inspected her friend for any sign of injury. She looked OK. Coral patted her friend's head. Her long blonde hair was a tangled, windswept knot, but the rest of her head seemed to be in good shape. She zoomed in on her friend's face with its puffy, red eyes and cheeks drenched in tears.

"Why are you crying?" she pleaded. Nicks had refused to tell her anything on the phone

7

– she'd only said that she had the worst news ever and that they should meet at the beach hut immediately.

Finally Nicks took a very deep breath. "My mum has been offered a new job!" she cried out.

Coral stared and blinked.

Nicks took a second deep breath. "And the job is in a town almost five hours away from Sunday Harbour!"

A new job... in a town almost five hours away? Coral gasped (it had taken a few moments for the awful news to make sense). "Is she actually going to take it?"

"I think she just might! She says it seems too good to pass up. She thinks she may never get an opportunity like this one again." The words tumbled out one after another.

Thoughts of endless days without Nicks spread through Coral's head. Suddenly her dry eyes sprang a leak. The tears spilled over her eyelids and landed on her cheeks with a splat. It really was the worst news ever.

"But what about you? And me? And us?"

"That's exactly what I said," groaned Nicks.

The girls hugged fiercely on the patch of sand directly in front of Coral Hut while Romeo gave a woeful whine. He was a small chocolate and white terrier with a very big heart.

"Come on, let's go inside," sniffed Coral, who was not usually the sensible one of the two, but today felt that she had to look after her best friend.

Nicks nodded and allowed herself to be led up the deck steps. Coral kept her jaw firm as she unlocked the beach hut's narrow double doors. A few determined tears tipped down her face but she swiped them away. Quickly she pulled out a couple of deckchairs and, grabbing one of the soft woollen candy-striped throws, dragged the whole lot out on to the deck.

"Sit," she said.

And they did, facing the gleaming silver ocean. Coral draped the throw over their knees and took her best friend's hand in her own. They sat that way for a few moments, not saying anything. Coral was trying desperately hard to be grown-up and brave for her friend's sake, but it was proving difficult. All she could think about was a Sunday Harbour without Nicks. And what about the Cupid Company they had set up together at Coral Hut? They were Cupid's co-workers – the best matchmaking team ever. Their motto was *All for love and love for all*. But a team needed at least two people. Coral shook her head to scatter the sad thoughts that were collecting like puddles. Squeezing Nicks's hand, she stared out at the horizon.

"Your mum hasn't quite made her mind up yet, has she?" she asked.

"Well, no, not fully," replied Nicks.

"So we still have a chance of persuading her to stay then?"

Nicks shrugged half-heartedly. "I guess so."

"Then that's what we'll do – we'll just have to find a way to get her to stay in Sunday Harbour!" Coral had an excellent imagination; she was never one to be outdone. Romeo yapped his agreement, like he understood everything, and Coral rubbed the fur between his ears thoughtfully. *But how…?*

"But how?" cried Nicks.

Coral coughed in a serious sort of way. "Well, we will… mmm. We could… um. How about we hide her car keys!"

Nicks frowned.

"No, that's just silly," added Coral before her friend could answer. "Well, how about sending your mum a pretend letter saying that the job has gone to someone else?"

Nicks shrugged and then shook her head.

"Yes, you're right – too deceitful," agreed

11

Coral. "Erm, you could beg and plead for her to stay?" she added hopefully.

"I've tried that one already," grumbled Nicks.

The morning air had been very still, but just at that moment a gust of wind sprang up out of nowhere. It tugged at the girls' hair and swirled around the deck, yanking at the Cupid Company poster taped to door. The poster fluttered to the floor like an autumn leaf. The wind disappeared and Romeo barked.

Coral stared at the poster. "I'VE GOT IT!" she cried out, grinning at the heavens. If they were Cupid's co-workers, then Aphrodite – the goddess of love – had just sent them a very clear instruction. Coral turned to face her friend with enormous moon eyes and a big smile. "How about the Cupid Company makes it their mission to find your mum the perfect partner. If she falls in love she'll never ever *ever* want to leave Sunday Harbour!" Coral punched the air determinedly. There really was nothing more powerful than love. It had been known to change lives.

Nicks straightened up immediately. Her head tilted from side to side as she considered this suggestion. And then she turned to face Coral. Her frown had turned itself upside down.

So Coral smiled too.

Nicks grinned.

Coral grinned.

"MAG-NIF-ICENT!" they both shouted out at once. And then they hugged (only this time it was out of happiness). It was time for the Cupid Company to work its magic.

shipmates

Nicks jumped to her feet and the throw slipped to the floor. She didn't give it a second glance. An organiser by nature, she now had the biggest Cupid Company assignment of their matchmaking careers to plot and plan. And as it was her mum they would be matchmaking, everything had to be very carefully considered.

She rushed inside the beach hut for her

clipboard and the file of completed Cupid Company questionnaires. All she had to do was search through them to find Mr Perfect. Except the file was not where she'd left it, neatly stored inside the white wicker basket. Now where could Coral have put it?

Nicks stood up and stuck her head out through the open door. Coral was leaning over the deck's railing and talking to a middle-aged man and woman who were standing on the deck of the glossy red beach hut next door – the hut that belonged to the famous crime thriller writer, J.D. 'Doctor Death' Hatchett. He'd left Sunday Harbour with a 'To Let' sign on the red hut's door, so there was a good chance that the couple were the red beach hut's new occupants. Nicks joined Coral out on the deck and waved politely.

"This is my very best friend Nicks," announced Coral in a loud voice. And then she turned to Nicks. "This is Meredith and

Malcolm. The name Meredith means 'protector of the sea'."

"Oh, OK!" smiled Nicks. "Hello!"

The protector of the sea grinned broadly and waved. She was slim with black-grey wispy hair that wafted on the sea breeze like tumbleweed. Malcolm was a small man with wide shoulders, thick legs and a very kind face.

"We're marine scientists," he revealed proudly.

"This beach hut is our research base for the rest of the summer," joined in Meredith. "Our mission is to convince the world – scientific and otherwise – to change the name of the starfish to the 'sea star', because, well, *it's not a fish!* It doesn't even look like a fish."

Both girls stared silently at their new neighbours. Could you do that? Just tell the world to just change the name of something? If so, Coral had a few suggestions of her own

– like seahorse, dragonfly and catfish. None of them made sense either. She imagined creating public campaigns to lobby for—

Suddenly an elbow lodged in her side. Nicks and their new neighbours were all staring at her expectantly.

"That's a really good idea!" she replied enthusiastically. But she didn't mention the seahorses, dragonflies or catfish just yet.

"It is?" squawked Nicks.

"Great news!" replied Meredith. "Collecting washed-up marine matter from the shoreline can be very exciting. And we could really do with the help."

Coral stared and shrugged. She'd missed something; she just wasn't quite sure what it was yet.

Nicks huffed. Not that she really minded helping their new neighbours clear up, but they had to get her mum to fall in love. Everything depended on it! There really was no time for anything else.

"Well, we'd better say goodbye," she said with a gentle smile. "We have lots to do."

"Yes, lots and lots," agreed Coral.

And, waving goodbye, Nicks and Coral disappeared inside Coral Hut, where they fished out the file of completed Cupid Company questionnaires that was lodged in between the books of romantic poetry on the shelf. Coral then settled into a deckchair beside Nicks and opened the file.

"So let's start by making a shortlist of perfect partners for your mum."

Nicks nodded. "We must find someone who is kind, clever, funny and handsome."

"Right," agreed Coral as she flicked through the questionnaires on file. "Kind. Clever. Funny. Handsome..." She flicked some more. "We seem to have a shortage of questionnaires."

"Pass me that," snapped Nicks. She was usually a very patient sort, but today her nerves made her nervy. They could not mess this one up. So she flicked left and flicked right. Questionnaires covered in scribble floated on the breeze. Finally Nicks glanced up. "There's no one kind, clever, funny or handsome enough!"

The girls slumped. Even Romeo's hairy chin dipped to the floor. But inspiration was not long in coming. Coral squinted while she waited for a new idea to land in her head. One always came. Finally she sat bolt upright.

"This Cupid Company case is not like any other we've ever had before, is it?"

Nicks shook her head in agreement. *"This one is the most important case by far."*

"Usually our clients come to us looking for love," continued Coral thoughtfully. "But your mum... well, she's not really looking for love, is she?"

Nicks nodded glumly. "I think she'd try her hardest not to fall in love right now. All she can think about is that daft new job."

"So we can't ask your mum to complete a questionnaire. But that's OK, you know her better than anybody, right? You know her likes and dislikes."

"Well, sort of." Nicks thought about her mum. Her mum was just... *her mum.* "She really hasn't had many boyfriends, you know," she admitted.

Coral gave her chin a scratch. "She married your dad, that's a start."

"My parents got divorced."

"So you see – that's a start! We'll look for someone who is *not* like your dad."

Nicks frowned. She thought her dad was kind, clever, funny and handsome. "Maybe we should try and find someone who Mum has something in common with – you know, like a shared hobby."

"Good idea! So what are your mum's hobbies, apart from the post office?"

"The post office is where she works, Coral – it's not a hobby." Nicks fell silent and chewed her bottom lip for a few thoughtful moments. "She does like genealogy."

"That's probably why she works at the post office," replied Coral matter-of-factly. "What better place to collect stamps."

"Duh! Genealogy is when you trace your family tree and make heritage scrapbooks and collect heirlooms and stuff," explained Nicks.

"Oh, right." Coral was surprised. That all sounded too much like hard work. She was already thinking about other ideas. "Wouldn't it be brilliant if we could contact your mum's school sweetheart! You never know, maybe he's single too?" Her eyes were misty with the possibility of it all. *The only thing better than love was long-lost love.*

"My dad was her school sweetheart," harrumphed Nicks.

"Right – well there's only one thing left to do then," declared Coral hurriedly. "We have to find out what other things she's into. That might give us a clue as to what kind of man we should find her. We have to go to your house and do some of our own investigating.

We may only get one crack at this, so Mr Perfect had better be Mr Perfect! We'll flip through photo albums. We'll dig in old shoeboxes and look under the bed. We'll poke about in desk drawers and page through your mum's recipe books. We'll check her diary and even listen in on her phone calls. *This* is how we'll find out about her hobbies and interests!" Coral was excited by the mystery of it all, but Nicks was still stuck at recipe books.

"What do recipes have to do with finding Mr Perfect?"

"That's how we find out what her favourite foods are," replied Coral with an *isn't-it-obvious* face. "We need to know exactly what she likes and what she dislikes. What are her favourite things in the world? What are her hopes and dreams? But she must not find out what we're up to."

Nicks stared at her friend. When did getting her mum to fall in love turn into a top-secret spying operation? But then they were desperate. She shrugged.

Coral stood up, glanced about, and checked her watch. "I've got a dentist appointment. My mum will kill me if I'm late. We'll make contact at your house at say – oh-eleven-thirty-seven-a.m."

"I have no idea what that means, Coral."

Coral glanced about again, trying to contain her eagerness. "That means I'll meet you at your house this morning at thirty-seven minutes past eleven," she explained patiently to her friend, who obviously was not very good at this sort of thing. But Coral had always been a fan of James Bond films. She understood that they were now *secret* agents of love.

"Right, well, I'll hang out here for a while longer," replied Nicks.

"OK, fine." Coral kept her voice low and hoarse. "And I'll see you you-know-where at you-know-when. She winked and was gone.

Partners in crime

Coral arrived at Nicks's house at twenty minutes past twelve o'clock, but that was only because her mum had insisted on popping into the chemist after the dentist. But that was OK; it had worked out for the best in the end. Coral had spent that time in the fancy-dress shop three doors down from the chemist.

"Hey, Nicks!" she hissed as she hopped excitedly from one foot to the other. "Is your mum around?"

"She's upstairs, but she's leaving soon."

Coral grinned. "Perfect! Look what I have for us." She rattled a paper carrier bag printed with the words FANCY PANTS.

"Erm, a pair of fancy pants?" replied Nicks nervously. Her best friend was known to have some wild ideas.

Coral frowned. Her best friend could be odd at times. "Nope. I got us a pair of wigs." She opened the bag and removed one blonde and one curly reddish-brown wig. "They're for us, so that we can conduct our research without being noticed."

"Without being noticed by who?" wondered Nicks out loud.

"By your mum, of course! She must not know what we're up to, remember? And Sunday Harbour is a small town. So these will be perfect." She passed Nicks the wig that was long and blonde.

"They would be perfect, I guess," replied Nicks, "except have you noticed one thing?" She put the wig on her head.

Coral stared and blinked at her friend, who did not look very different at all. Nicks's own hair was long and blonde too. So she whipped the wig from her friend's head and handed her the wig that was reddish-brown and curly and a surprisingly good match to her own hair instead.

Nicks pressed this wig firmly on to her head and stared silently at Coral for a few moments. "There, now you'll look like me and I'll look like you. That should trick my mum."

Coral made a 'humph' sort of sound through her nostrils. Nicks wasn't being as grateful as Coral had imagined she'd be. Perhaps she should have got her the blue beehive – that would have shown her! But there wasn't any time to think any more about that now as suddenly Nicks's mum appeared at the door to the kitchen.

"Hello, Coral, dear," she chimed sweetly as she reached for her car keys hanging on a hook.

Coral shoved the blonde wig under her top. "Hi, Mrs Waterman," she replied.

"I do wish you'd call me Maggie," replied Nicks's mum. "What's that under your top, Coral?"

"Oh, this?" Coral patted her round soft belly. "Too many treats," she chuckled.

Maggie Waterman raised an eyebrow and made a face like she suspected something was up. But she didn't ask any further questions and simply kissed the tops of the girls' heads instead. "All right then, you two, be good, and I'll see you later." And then she was gone.

"I bet she's off to meet someone about that new job she's after," growled Coral, like it was an unforgivable offence.

"Actually she's off to the post office," replied Nicks, who was still holding the wig she'd hidden behind her back. "Now, where do we start?"

Coral stared around the kitchen. "We might as well start in here," she suggested.

Nicks deposited the reddish-brown wig on the countertop. They had to learn everything possible about her mum if they were going to find the perfect Mr Perfect. And the decorative bowl on top of the microwave seemed like a good place to start. It wasn't long before she held her hand in the air victoriously.

"Ticket stubs for the Sea Life Aquarium!" she announced, smiling. It had been a great day out – her mum did love the ocean and dolphins.

Coral grinned. "Brilliant – maybe Mr Perfect also loves fish and stuff!" She returned to her own exploring and found the door to a large cupboard beneath the stairs. Inside was a lady's bicycle with two flat tyres and cobwebbed spokes. There was also a tennis racket with broken strings and an abdominal exerciser with rusty hinges. These were excellent clues as to what Maggie Waterman did *not* enjoy. She turned to Nicks, who had her nose stuck in a book called *Recipes for Every Day of the Year*.

Her friend glanced up from her reading and nodded. "The pasta recipe pages show the most wear and tear. Mum does like pasta."

Coral drummed her fingers on her chin and gave this some thought. "Pasta is Italian food. And Mr Selvaggio at Deli Antonia is Italian. He must be very lonely since Mrs Selvaggio passed away. So that's another place for us to visit."

"What is?" asked Nicks, who no longer had any idea what Coral was talking about.

"Deli Antonia! Now, shall we head upstairs?"

Nicks led the way to a bedroom that was decorated in white with a small gold chandelier and a large gilt-edged mirror over a dresser.

"This room is lovely," ooh'd Coral. "It's so girly and romantic."

"My mum does enjoy decorating. She

buys all the latest interior decorating magazines."

"So that's another thing then!" cheered Coral, who was really starting to enjoy this snooping... or *investigating*. "If there's a kind, clever, funny, handsome, pasta-loving interior decorator in Sunday Harbour – we will find him!"

Nicks was finally beginning to believe that this research wasn't such a bad idea after all. "Come on – I'll get the photo albums out," she said as she reached beneath the bed for a large box with a label that read FAMILY PHOTOS. Inside the box were three matching photo albums. Hoisting one out, she clambered on top of her mum's white bedspread. "Now, what exactly are we looking for?"

Coral joined her friend on the bed and nestled in close. Reaching over, she turned to the first page of the photo album. There were snaps of Nick's mum when she was younger, taking part in various stage productions. Coral jabbed a finger at one of the photographs.

"Look – see, your mum obviously loves the theatre."

Nicks seemed surprised. She'd really had no idea. Her mum had always kept very busy... well, just being her mum.

"So maybe Mr Perfect could be a member of Sunday Harbour's amateur dramatics society?" suggested Coral as she turned the pages of the photo album.

The next set of photographs consisted of beach shots that were so old they were black and white. These would have been taken way before Maggie Waterman's time. The women in the pictures wore swimming costumes that had skirts attached and the men walked about in straw hats. Coral didn't like to imagine a world without colour and was about to turn the page when one particular photo caught her eye. It showed a row of beach huts that looked remarkably similar to Sunday Harbour's own row of beach huts. Coral paused and peered closely. Sand dunes rose up in the background. There was a promenade. And a sign beneath a lamp post that advised: PEDESTRIANS AND BICYCLES ONLY. Sunday Harbour's promenade had an identical sign, in exactly the same place!

Coral's nose was now practically touching the album as she scanned the rest of the photographs closely. One photograph three down and two across suddenly seemed to jump out at her. It was mounted with a narrow cardboard edging and somebody had written an inscription in capitals along the bottom of the cardboard mount. OUR LOVELY BEACH HUT, it said. This particular photo showed a close up of the front of a beach hut with two young girls standing on the hut's deck, smiling and holding hands. Like the beach bathers in the other black and white photographs, they also wore old-fashioned swimming costumes and had heads of matching corkscrew curls decorated with large droopy bows. The girls were probably about twelve years old, although the bows made them look a little younger. Coral chuckled. She was twelve years old and couldn't imagine wearing big old bows in her hair!

And then she noticed two more details. The first was that both girls had shiny, heart-shaped pendants on silver chains around their necks. And secondly, there was a number five nailed to the wood directly above the beach hut's doors. The tail of the number five – which was supposed to curve like a half-O shape – was cut short. It was missing. Well, the end bit of it was missing. Coral gasped. She'd seen that half-missing number five a trillion times before. *They were looking at an ancient photograph of Coral Hut!*

"What's the matter?" asked Nicks.

Coral tapped the photograph with her

finger and made strange gurgling noises. Try as she might, she couldn't get any words out.

Nicks followed Coral's finger and stared closely at the photograph for a few moments. "Hey, I think that's Coral Hut!" she cried out.

"I know!" Finally Coral could talk.

Nicks peered even closer. "Wowzers – imagine that. I wonder who those two girls are?"

Coral nodded excitedly. "Me too. But just as importantly – why does your mum have an old photograph of Coral Hut?"

"It probably wasn't called Coral Hut back then," suggested Nicks in her usual rational sort of way.

Coral did not think that this was relevant. "This is an album of family photographs, right?" she said instead. "So could this... do you think this means that someone in your family owned Coral Hut once upon a time?"

Nicks raised an eyebrow and smiled. "Imagine that," she cooed and tapped her chin. "In that case, maybe Coral Hut was once called Nicks's Hut? Or Nicola Hut, even. It is a family name, you know."

Coral swiftly shook the suggestion from her head. "I doubt it. And it doesn't really matter anyway. It won't help us to find Mr Perfect." She was about to turn the album page, but Nicks wasn't quite ready to move on just yet.

"I think we should find out. It would be really interesting. I mean – imagine if my ancestors spent their summers at our hut too."

"We really should be focusing on Mr Perfect," Coral said gruffly.

"I know. But we could do both. Maybe my mum will know. After all, she's interested in family trees and stuff."

"You can't ask your mum!" Coral bleated. "If she suspects anything she'll be on her guard and it will make getting her to fall in love even more difficult."

Nicks frowned. Coral did have a point. Perhaps it was better to play things safe. "I know – we'll ask your mum instead. After all, you must have received some sort of ownership documents when you inherited the hut from your Great-Aunt Coral."

"I guess," admitted Coral, who was still not madly keen on the idea of Coral Hut being known as anything other than Coral Hut. Ever. "OK – we'll ask my mum," she finally agreed. "But for now we should focus on finishing our investigation."

Nicks nodded eagerly and reached for the notebook and pen on her mum's bedside table. And then she began scribbling. She was making a list of all the leads they had for Mr Perfect. There was the aquarium... and Mr Selvaggio at Deli Antonia... and the local theatre... maybe an interior decorator...

Coral leaned over and peered at the list.

And then she smiled. Finally they had some sort of plan. Now all they had to do was find Mr Perfect and get Cupid to take careful aim. And then Nicks would never leave Sunday Harbour. Now how difficult could that really be?

together forever

"So what exactly do we do when we get to Deli Antonia?" Nicks wondered out loud.

"Well, we could ask Mr Selvaggio to fill in a Cupid Company questionnaire," suggested Coral. "But that takes time, which we don't have, so maybe we should just ask him plenty of relevant questions instead. We urgently need to find out if he's our Mr Perfect. After all, you can't build a marriage on pasta alone."

"Marriage?" squawked Nicks. "Who said anything about my mum getting married?"

"Well, isn't that what happens when you fall in love? You get married," explained Coral. But Nicks didn't look very convinced. In fact, she looked like she didn't want to think about it at all. Tightening her grip on Romeo's lead, she quickened her step. It was a warm day and they'd already been walking for a while, so Nicks thought about a long, cold drink instead.

There was the usual crowd gathering outside the Sea Life Aquarium; afternoons meant feeding time for the bigger fish and it was always worth queuing for. But today there seemed to be a different sort of commotion going on. The girls looked closer until they saw what it was that was causing all the fuss. And then they saw them – Meredith and Malcolm at the front of the crowd, handing out bits of paper and shouting about something. The girls moved closer.

"Come and see the sea star exhibition," hollered Meredith to the crowd.

"And discover why the starfish is really a sea star," added Malcolm with just as much enthusiasm.

Meredith noticed the girls and waved them over merrily. "Isn't this great!" she cheered. "We've really drawn a crowd."

Coral didn't have the heart to tell her that there was usually a bunch of people waiting to see the big fish get fed. She smiled instead.

"Would you like a free pass to see the sea star exhibition?" offered Malcolm. "After all, we are neighbours." He chuckled and Meredith chuckled like this was really quite funny.

"Erm, we're just off... on an errand for Nicks's mum," white-lied Coral.

Nicks nodded, adding, "But could we have two free passes for tomorrow instead?" It was a Plan B, just in case Mr Selvaggio was not Mr Perfect after all.

40

"Alrighty!" agreed Meredith. "And don't forget there's the Sea Life Aquarium Open Day coming up soon."

The girls nodded with interest. The Aquarium Open Day was something they looked forward to every year.

"And you be sure to join us on a beach scavenge sometime soon," concluded Malcolm. "Dawn is such a dazzling time of day; we find such interesting marine life along the shoreline."

Both Coral and Nicks nodded once more, even though the mention of the word 'dawn' made them feel very sleepy. Just then a man with a large belly covered in a stretched Hawaiian cotton shirt squeezed past Nicks. He was trailed by four small, round children carrying ice creams. They all shuffled past and joined the queue for the aquarium. They were followed by three sauntering surfer dudes who left wafts of coconut oil in their wake. And then an old man wearing holey clothes and a captain's cap came hobbling along, carrying his stinky bait box. The day was hot, noisy and aromatic. There was nothing quite like summertime in Sunday Harbour. Nicks was more aware of this than anybody.

Finally Coral and Nicks and Meredith and Malcolm waved goodbye and went their separate ways. The marine scientists continued handing out flyers and the girls pressed on in the direction of Mr Selvaggio and Deli Antonia. Nicks had a very determined look in her eye.

The deli wasn't very busy when they arrived and the girls peered through the large shopfront window while they secured Romeo's lead to a post outside. Inside were two old ladies in tortoiseshell glasses seated at a small table near the wall. A man in a suit was hunched over the glass deli counter, studying the meat, cheese and pickles and making a small 'mmm' sound, like he was running off a generator. Behind the counter a short, dark man wearing a bright white apron stood and waited, silent and expectant. It was Mr Selvaggio. Both girls stopped and stared at him closely. He still had all his hair, which was slicked back with some type of oil. He skin was soft and a little saggy, but it was a nice nutty colour, and his moustache was very neatly trimmed. And he had warm black eyes that almost seemed to twinkle.

Finally the man in the suit made up his mind and barked out his order to Mr Selvaggio, who nimbly wrapped some salami slices in brown paper and filled a small plastic pot with olives. The girls turned to each other. *This man was efficient!* That was the great thing about being best friends – they didn't always need words. Mr Selvaggio then popped the salami and olives into a bag and finally added a small crusty roll to its contents. He handed the bag over with a friendly smile.

"The bread is on-a the house," he said with a soft Italian accent.

The girls turned to each other once again. *And generous!*

The man in the suit left Deli Antonia with a smile, leaving Mr Selvaggio free to focus on the girls. "And what-a may I do for-a you?" he said.

"Hiya," said Coral while Nicks stood there silently. She suddenly felt nervous. *What if Mr Selvaggio did marry her mum?*

Mr Selvaggio smiled while he waited patiently for their order. But Coral's mind had gone blank. *She should have prepared a few questions!* So she tried to focus on what sort of man they were looking for. *Ah yes, someone who was kind, clever, funny, handsome.*

"So, Mr Selvaggio," she began, "do you do any charity work?"

Mr Selvaggio looked confused. "Uh, well we do try-a to collect for the Seawatch

Foundation," he stammered as he pointed to the plastic boat-shaped moneybox on the countertop.

Coral beamed at Nicks and turned to face Mr Selvaggio once more. "And what is the square root of 37?" She didn't know the answer to this herself, but she hoped that Mr Selvaggio would answer very quickly because that would be telling enough.

Mr Selvaggio's forehead scrunched up while he gave this some silent thought.

"OK – what is the capital of Italy then?" Coral blurted out.

Mr Selvaggio looked instantly relieved. "That would'a be Rome!"

Coral clapped. He definitely knew that one! "Now, tell us your favourite joke, please."

Mr Selvaggio looked very confused. "But-a why?"

"Why?" echoed Coral. "Well... because... because the great thing about living in Sunday Harbour is our community spirit.

Everyone knows everybody else. And we – my good friend NICKS WATERMAN and I – just love getting to know people better."

Mr Selvaggio could not argue with that. "My favourite-a joke..." he considered, looking up at the ceiling. And then he began. "Knock-a knock-a."

"Who's there?" replied both girls eagerly (even Nicks was feeling Coral's community spirit speech).

"Tuna."

"Tuna who?"

"Tuna your radio down, I'm trying to get some sleep!" Mr Selvaggio chuckled.

Both girls stood there blinking.

Tuna your round radio down...? Coral turned to look at Nicks.

At least the joke kind of works with an Italian accent, that has to count for something! And he obviously has a very good sense of humour!

They turned back to Mr Selvaggio and

laughed too. But Coral wasn't done interrogating yet. Nicks, meanwhile, had just noticed a thin, shiny gold wedding band on Mr Selvaggio's ring finger. She stared. *Maybe he just hadn't got around to taking it off yet. After all, it couldn't have been easy for him when his wife passed away.* Nicks decided to push the thought from her mind.

"So what sort of things do you enjoy doing?" continued Coral, who was too busy with the verbal questionnaire to notice any gold ring.

Meanwhile, Nicks's eyes crept up to the counter behind Mr Selvaggio. There was a very large, very shiny chrome coffee machine with funnels and drip trays. There were labelled canisters filled with different kinds of coffee as well as sugar. There were boxes of mocha sticks stuffed with chocolate. And then Nicks's gaze landed on a large glass dome over a plate of what appeared to be square biscuits studded with dried fruit. A sign next to the dome of biscuits read:

HANDMADE FRUIT BISCOTTI – FRESHLY BAKED BY MRS ANTONIA SELVAGGIO

Nicks's gaze settled on Mr Selvaggio's wedding ring once again. She looked back to the sign advertising the fruit biscotti. And then it all became very clear. Coral had got it all wrong. Mrs Selvaggio was obviously alive and well and very well; it must have been Mr Selvaggio's *mother* who had passed away.

"Coral!" she hissed.

But Coral was too busy with her interrogation. She'd just remembered Nicks's mum's bicycle with the cobweb spokes and the tennis racket with its broken strings and thought she'd better be more specific with her questions. "Do you enjoy playing sport, Mr Selvaggio?"

"CORAL!"

Coral smiled apologetically at Mr Selvaggio and then faced her best friend with a glare. *Can't you see I'm trying to find Mr Perfect!*

Nicks made big eyes at the ring finger on her hand. She then nodded a few times in Mr Selvaggio's direction.

But Coral was not taking any notice. "And what about the theatre – when was the last time you attended, Mr Selvaggio?"

"You probably took your wife along with you, didn't you, Mr Selvaggio?" interrupted Nicks with an uneasy smile.

"Yes, you—" began Coral. And then her head quickly snapped back in Nicks's direction. "Now, Nicks," she said kindly, "that's just being silly."

Mr Selvaggio looked very bewildered, but seemed relieved to be able to answer at least one question directly. "Actually, my-a wife does enjoy-a the theatre very-a much," he admitted. "And she's just-a in the back. I call her and you can ask for yourself!" His face

49

was desperate, like he'd do almost anything to get out of answering any more of these annoying girls' questions.

Coral stood ramrod straight with her eyes in a wide O-shape. Her jaw flapped as she struggled to find words to speak. So Nicks stepped in.

"Oh, that's OK, Mr Selvaggio, we've really got to get going anyway. But it's been great getting to know you. And we're sorry about your mum."

She pressed a hand into Coral's back and gently bulldozed her in the direction of the door. Coral was stammering but making very little sense, although at one point she did mumble something that sounded like *it must be a miracle...*

stalemate

Nicks patted her pocket, the one containing the two free passes to the sea star exhibition at the aquarium. Yesterday's visit to Deli Antonia had been a disaster with embarrassing consequences. Not that Coral really saw it like this. She was rather indignant about the whole affair, almost as if Mr Selvaggio had tricked them by being married all along. *So much for Sunday*

Harbour community spirit, she harrumphed.

"Come on!" urged Nicks.

Coral ambled along with her hands buried deep inside her pockets and kicked a smooth pebble.

"Oh, get over it, Coral. So you didn't know there were two Mrs Selvaggios – it's no biggie."

Actually, inside Coral felt disappointed. She definitely did not want Nicks to leave Sunday Harbour and she'd really (really really) hoped that this would be an easy Cupid Company case. But so far it was proving to be anything but easy!

"Here's your pass," said Nicks as they reached the aquarium admissions booth.

Coral took the pass from her friend and handed it over to the lady wearing a Sally Seal hat and T-shirt. The lady noticed Coral noticing her outfit and whispered conspiratorially, "My name really is Sally – isn't that cool! We've all got our special aquarium names." She pointed to Gary Great White standing nearby, handing out balloons. And then she laughed and clapped her palms together like a seal.

Coral stared at the woman. *She really does throw herself into her job*, she thought. Coral never did anything in half measures either, and suddenly she applauded the woman's efforts (but not in a seal sort of way).

Nicks, meanwhile, was all business as she carefully scrutinised their surroundings. "Now, I suppose we can assume that everyone who is here loves the ocean, right?"

Coral nodded, vaguely distracted by Gary Great White who was doing shark impressions. He was really quite good. So Coral made a shark fin with her hand and held it on top of her head. Gary Great White certainly seemed to appreciate her efforts and took another great big shark bite out of the fresh air. And then Coral spotted Chris Crab.

"Oh, would you stop it!" snapped Nicks as she slapped Coral's raised scissor-fingers. "Can we just get on? Now we just have to find a man who is kind, clever, funny and handsome. And not married."

Ahead of them was a board with a colourful map of the aquarium's layout. Nicks studied it closely while she decided on a plan. Up ahead was the Touch Tank. Then to the left was the twenty-metre-long underwater tunnel with its moving walkway. To the right was the half-moon shark tank. And further along was Reef Magic – Nurseries of the Seas. The aquarium wasn't all indoors though. Visitors could go outside to admire the dolphin pool and seal enclosures.

Coral was reading from the board too, and suddenly she pointed a finger at the area called Coral Bay.

"That's my favourite place," she ooh'd.

Nicks stared at her friend and then returned to the map. *It was only Coral's*

favourite because her name *was featured in the title.* "Come on – let's head for the Touch Tank," she said, a little more sharply that she'd intended. It was in the opposite direction to Coral Bay.

They hadn't walked for more than a minute or two when they were approached by Julie Jellyfish. Her arms were stiff and bent and trembled at the elbows. Coral grinned and did her own jellyfish impression, which involved wobbling her head too (something she felt Julie's impression was missing). Julie was obviously impressed, because she laughed and added the head-wobble to her act as well.

"Welcome to the Sea Life Aquarium – home to global marine life," warbled Julie Jellyfish as she handed both girls a shiny printed leaflet. "Would you like to adopt a sea creature?"

"Er…" Coral stared at the leaflet and read through the list of sea creatures up for adoption. She couldn't see her mum letting her keep a hammerhead shark. Or a leatherback turtle. A pair of sea otters was probably out of the question too. The most she could probably do was a clownfish – a little swimmer like Nemo. But this didn't seem to be on the list. She was about to raise this point with Julie Jellyfish, but Nicks had just noticed a board listing the feeding times. She pointed to it, checked her watch and smiled at Julie Jellyfish while she shoved the leaflet into her pocket.

"We've got to hurry if we're going to make feeding time!"

So Coral followed Nicks over to the chest-high tank with a man inside wearing bright orange plastic waders and holding a bowl filled with food. A crowd had already gathered, but that was good; it was the crowd Coral and Nicks were interested in. They screened the hairy heads – searching for a handsome candidate for Mr Perfect. There were a lot of old people and a lot of young people in the crowd, but there weren't many in between.

Coral elbowed Nicks and whispered, "Perhaps we should move on."

Nicks nodded like it was a good idea. They wandered through the aquarium – past a cafe called Fish Fingers and the half-moon shark tank and the aquarium novelty shop, but they could really only focus on the aquarium visitors. It was, after all, why they were here.

They came across a large poster inviting them to meet the new aquarium manager, which seemed a good idea. But when they got to his office, it turned out the manager was off supervising the repair of a leak in a tank of electric eels, so they continued on their way. Finally they came to Coral Bay, which was quite simply a tank packed with different types of coral and thousands of small, brightly coloured fish. Coral Bay did not draw as many spectators, although the girls did notice *one* possible candidate for Mr Perfect.

This man wasn't very tall, but he had a kind smile and was dressed well. And then they noticed the camera around his neck.

"A tourist – no good," murmured Nicks. She wanted to *stay* in Sunday Harbour. So they continued on to the Touch Tank, which was just a short distance away. This was the attraction that had drawn the largest crowd. Nicks gazed around her with eyes like a hawk. Coral stared with eyes on stalks. And then Nicks nudged Coral. Coral nodded. She'd seen him too.

There, on the other side of the Touch Tank, was a tall man with black hair and friendly eyes. He gazed into the water intently and then turned to the teenage boys around him. He was clearly a teacher on a field trip and the boys seemed to be having a great time.

Turning back to the Touch Tank, he pointed out some of the sea creatures swimming or lolling about in the cool, clear water. The teenagers seemed especially drawn to the stingrays with their elegant wings that rippled like grey, velvety cloaks in the water. Coral and Nicks moved into position, right beside the field trip group, and watched closely. The stingrays were captivating, with winning little smiles.

Potential Mr Perfect looked from the teenage boys to the stingrays. And then he slowly slipped his right arm into the cool water. Bending forward as far as he could, his hand reached towards the stingrays. The teenage boys fell silent and, like Coral and Nicks, all leaned forward – ever so slightly – watching, waiting. Potential Mr Perfect's hand was heading for one of the largest stingrays in the tank. The stingray remained still and patient. And then it twitched.

Potential Mr Perfect leaped back and howled with fright. He clutched his heart and howled a few more times, but in a rather high-pitched, girly sort of way, like he was having a heart attack. Some of the passers-by clearly thought he might be and moved closer with looks of concern on their faces. But the teenage boys knew exactly what had happened and they howled with laughter. They laughed so hard they bent at the waist and thumped their knees or the backs of their friends. They laughed so hard they cried. And while all this went on, poor old Potential Mr Perfect still clutched his chest and breathed like he was going to have a baby.

"Come on, Coral," grumbled Nicks. "He's not our man."

PEN PALS

The girls regrouped at Coral Hut the following day, but Coral was not her usual bold, brave and breezy self. Today she felt a little low. After all, they still weren't any closer to rooting out Mr Perfect.

"Cheer up – we have never failed before," said Nicks as she tried to jolly her friend along. Today it was her turn to be the positive one.

"I guess," mumbled Coral as she gave Romeo a cuddle. "But we don't have much time. We haven't even found Mr Perfect yet. And then we've still got to get your mum to fall in love with him."

"Hey-ho!" hollered an unexpected voice.

Both girls and pup glanced up to see Meredith and Malcolm heading up the beach towards Coral Hut. Meredith carried a small, silver bucket.

Romeo jumped to his feet and raced quick-as-a-blur down the hut steps and over to their new neighbours as if they were old friends. He then pranced about and walked backwards on his hind legs and did fancy figures of eight. Meredith giggled and clapped like she was most impressed.

Coral and Nicks watched the show and wondered what had got into Romeo. He didn't usually perform tricks – well, not without the promise of a very visible treat anyway. They were even more surprised when Romeo leaped into Meredith's arms. She nearly dropped her silver bucket, but quickly managed to balance small, hairy dog and bucket quite well.

Meredith was still smiling when she reached the top of the hut's stripy steps. "Look what I have here!" she announced, holding Romeo out like a prize before he slipped from her grip and settled into a deckchair. "I have a confession," she continued. "Your pup found Malcolm's stash of shortbread. He's a sucker for the stuff. Anyway, he ate the lot. I do hope the little guy wasn't sick."

Coral wasn't sure if the shortbread sucker was Malcolm or Romeo, but either way, it did not excuse Romeo's raid on their neighbour's treats.

"I'm very sorry," she apologised.

"Oh, it's all our fault," cooed Meredith. "Malcolm has a very bad habit of forgetting to put his snacks away when he's had enough.

So of course Romeo sniffed them out and came skipping over."

Meredith sent Malcolm a glare, so Coral thought she'd better glare at Romeo too. The chocolate and white pup rested a paw across his eyes and pretended to be asleep. Malcolm didn't seem particularly bothered either.

"Ooh, what is the Cupid Company?" asked Meredith suddenly. She'd just noticed the sign on the door of Coral Hut.

"Um, the Cupid Company..." sighed Coral miserably.

Nicks stared long and hard at her best friend, who was usually the cheeriest person around. She then curled an arm around her shoulders and gave her a cuddle. "We are the Cupid Company!" she announced brightly. "We're the best matchmakers around. We point love in the right direction. And we usually get it right – eventually." She smiled at Coral, who managed a very small smile in return.

"Our motto is *All for love and love for all*," Coral added with a smidgen of gusto. Nicks was relieved to see some of her best friend's optimism return.

"Matchmakers, huh?" commented Meredith. "That is interesting. Not that we'd be interested." And then she laughed and jerked a thumb towards Malcolm. "We're far too busy to look for love."

"TOO BUSY FOR LOVE?!" howled Coral and Nicks in unison. That was crazy talk.

"So you're not married then?" added Coral like it was the oddest thing ever.

"WHO, US?" cried Meredith and Malcolm at once.

"As if!" whooped Malcolm.

"Psssht!" wheezed Meredith.

"We're far too busy with our research to even think about romance. We're just good friends."

Coral and Nicks looked at each other and mused this over in silence for a few moments.

What a strange pair their neighbours were. *Research over romance?* But of course they didn't say anything of the sort out loud. They just nodded and smiled courteously.

"So how is the whole starfish thing going?" asked Nicks politely.

"You mean the sea star thing," Meredith corrected her. "Remember, the starfish is not a fish. So it should be called the sea star."

Coral nodded thoughtfully. She rather liked the idea of starting her own name-change campaign. Maybe she'd start with the word 'homework'. It would be much better off known as 'nowork'. Now that was the sort of word she would like to hear at the end of the school day—

"Hello, Coral!" called a voice. Coral turned to find her mum standing at the top of the hut's steps. She was carrying a small, padded, blue cooler bag. "You forgot your breakfast, darling."

Coral remembered; she'd been feeling far

too glum for breakfast that morning. But she was certainly feeling a bit brighter now. "Are those breakfast muffins?" she asked.

A nod of Coral's mum's head confirmed that they were. "With blueberries."

"Thanks, Mum. Oh, and this is Meredith and Malcolm – our new beach hut neighbours."

Everyone said hello and Meredith nattered some more about the sea star while Romeo sniffed at the blue cooler bag with a face that said that blueberries were not his favourite but they were better than nothing.

"Anyway," concluded Meredith with a sigh, just to prove how exhausting the sea star business really was, "we really should be going. We still have more beach specimens to collect today." She jiggled the silver bucket that was still in her hand, then disappeared with a wave.

"Meredith and Malcolm are just friends," Coral whispered hoarsely in her mum's direction (just in case marine scientists had super-charged hearing).

"That's nice," commented her mum.

"So they're not married," added Coral in a low voice. "They do research instead of romance."

Coral's mum nodded. "Oh, right."

But Nicks seemed to have other things on her mind. She hadn't forgotten about the black and white photograph of the beach hut that they'd found in her mum's album. It was a mystery she still wanted to get to the bottom of.

"How much do you know about the history of this beach hut?" she asked Coral's mum.

"What – other than it used to belong to Great-Aunt Coral?"

Nicks nodded.

"Not very much, really. I believe Great-Aunt Coral had it for many years. She inherited this hut, just like our own Coral did. And I suppose Great-Aunt Coral inherited it from someone in the family too... although I don't know this for certain."

"How could we find out?" wondered Nicks.

"There should be ownership records somewhere. Coral inherited this beach hut, but the ground it stands on actually belongs to the Council. They own the beach. Perhaps you could check with them."

Nicks nodded like it was a very good idea.

"Why are you so interested in the history of Coral Hut all of a sudden?"

Nicks's mouth stretched with a very small, secretive smile. But she didn't want to tell anybody else about the black and white photograph just yet. "These beach huts have been around for a while," she replied simply. "It would just be interesting to know, that's all."

Coral made a humph sound. *Nicola Hut indeed!*

"You know, your mum could probably help you to find out more, Nicks," suggested

Coral's mum. "She's used to researching history. You know how good she is with family trees and that sort of thing."

"Ask my mum? No, I don't think so," replied Nicks quickly. "This is er... something Coral and I want to do ourselves."

Coral rolled her eyes. *She wasn't that bothered really.* Nicks aimed an elbow at her ribs. "Owf! I mean – yes, this is something we want to do. And besides, Nicks's mum is far too busy contemplating her new job," she added sulkily.

"Her new job?" answered Coral's mum. "That is exciting! So is your mum finally going back to teaching? She always said she wanted to teach again some day."

"Teach?" echoed Nicks with giant goggle eyes. "Was my mum a teacher?"

Coral's mum smiled. "Yes, a long time ago – before you were born. She stopped teaching to take care of you."

"And now she works part-time at the post

office..." mumbled Nicks, who suddenly realised just how much of her mum's life revolved around her. *Was she very wrong for trying to get her mum to remain in Sunday Harbour?*

"Anyway, girls – thanks for the chit-chat – now I've got errands to run. Coral, be home for dinner, please. And Nicks, of course, you're welcome to join us. We're having meatloaf."

Romeo sat up and sniffed the air. Coral's mum bent low and patted his head. "And you're having beef biscuits."

Romeo slid back down on his belly and made a sad face. Not that Coral's mum noticed. She was already halfway down the hut's stripy steps.

Nicks turned to face Coral, who was standing motionless, her feet wide and her eyes wild. Even her hair seemed to be a little more crazy-curly than usual. "Hold on, Nicks," she said. "I think I'm about to have an Einstein moment."

Nicks stood silent and patient. She knew all about her best friend's Einstein moments. And they were not always something to get excited about.

"Mr Sparks!" cried Coral with her finger pointed high in the air like she was about to kebab a cloud. "Yes! He's the one!"

"The one for—"

But Coral's train of thought was not stopping at any stations. "*Mr Sparks is MR PERFECT!* Think about it. He's kind. He's quite funny – sometimes, when he's not ordering me to be quiet. He's sort of handsome... er, enough. I mean, he still grows his own hair and he's always very clean. And of course he's clever. You can't be headteacher without being clever. And he's definitely not married. Everyone knows that. But best of all, your mum and Mr Sparks have something humungous in common – they... "

"...ARE BOTH TEACHERS!" joined in Nicks triumphantly. She considered another excellent point in Mr Sparks's favour: Coral and Nicks had known him since forever. He'd been their headteacher since the day they had started school. He was as familiar and reliable as sunshine. He really was Mr Perfect. It seemed like maybe Coral had just experienced an Einstein moment after all...

a name is forever

"TO-TALLY BRILL-IANT!" cheered the girls.

"This has to be your greatest Einstein moment ever!" added Nicks merrily. Her best friend really was the *best* best friend in the entire town, country, planet and universe.

"Now we just have to decide on a plan of action."

Nicks nodded thoughtfully. "Of course, my mum has met Mr Sparks already..."

Coral bit her bottom lip and fiddled with her fingers. She was being just as thoughtful. "So we don't need to worry about awkward introductions... but we do need to get your mum and Mr Sparks to fall in love. So how do we do that?"

"We need to think extreme romance..."

"Quite right, we need to consider the greatest romances of all time." Both Coral and Nicks loved romantic films; they never missed a good one and often watched the very best ones a dozen times over.

"But the problem with romantic films," added Coral, "is that the guy and girl usually start off not liking each other very much at all."

"Mmm, that's true. And I think my mum likes Mr Sparks just fine."

"But that's good too, right?" guessed Coral. Nicks nodded her reply. "But we need a plan. Maybe we need to focus specifically on the best-ever romantic *moments* of all time? For example, sunsets – they are seriously romantic."

Nicks bobbed her chin in agreement. "Candlelight is romantic too. And soft music."

"What about a room filled with red roses?"

"And long strolls along the beach."

Coral tried to imagine Maggie Waterman and Mr Sparks together, walking along the beach. It created a strange sort of image in her head in which Mr Sparks was updating Maggie Waterman on Nicks's progress throughout the school term, like a very intimate parent–teacher meeting. Coral shook her head to clear it. She had to try and think of Mr Sparks the man, not Mr Sparks the headteacher.

"How would we even get them to agree to a walk along the beach together?" Nicks wondered. Her mum might think that was very weird indeed.

"Well, they wouldn't have to know. We could set them up... like a blind date...

except it would be a blind walk along the beach."

"Sounds dangerous," murmured Nicks. "No, maybe we should start off small. How about a group gathering of some sort?"

"A group gathering..." repeated Coral, slowly chewing her bottom lip. She scratched her chin. She tapped her foot. "Nope, I'm not getting anything," she finally said.

"Me neither," admitted Nicks. "We're trying too hard. We need to think about something else for a bit. Let's head over to the Council offices and see what we can find there. I still can't stop thinking about the old photograph of Coral Hut in my mum's photo album."

"I guess it would be interesting to know what tied your family to Coral Hut all those years ago," admitted Coral. *Even if she still wasn't wild about the Nicola Hut theory...*

Nicks jumped up. "Come on then!" Romeo was just as ready for a bit of action and he quickly landed on his paws and stood ready and alert with his tongue panting and tail wagging.

They set off, Nicks leading the way. They negotiated the promenade packed with jostling beach lovers. They cut through the old fish factory, which was now a shiny new fish restaurant called Fish. They arrived on the main street and marched past shop fronts and sidewalk cafes until finally they arrived at the Council offices, located in a white, square, double-storeyed building with cornflower-blue wooden shutters. There wasn't much in Sunday Harbour that wasn't pretty.

They climbed the steps and pushed through two large doors and came to a stop at the long wooden counter marked with a sign that said RECEPTION. The receptionist was a lady with pink nails and long hair piled high on her head. Coral stared. *Just how did she remain balanced with a tower of hair on top of her head like that?*

"Good morning," said Nicks in an officious sort of way. "We'd like to look at the records for the beach huts, please."

"What kind of records?" replied the receptionist.

Coral rested both elbows on the countertop. *And just how did her hair stay all the way up there? There were no visible hairclips...*

"The, uh... ownership records?" guessed Nicks uncertainly.

The receptionist nodded. The tower of hair nodded and teetered. But still it stayed firmly in place.

Coral leaned in closer. *Could it be a tower created out of hairspray? That would be remarkable...*

"What you'll need to do," continued the receptionist as she pointed with her pink fingernails, "is follow the corridor until you get to the fourth door on the right. Then you should ask for Mr Chattopadhyay."

Nicks smiled and nodded, keeping the name Mr Chattopadhyay on the tip of her tongue so that she would not forget it. She turned from the counter, but her best friend stayed firm and did not budge. So Nicks quietly kicked her ankles (she daren't speak a word – just in case she forgot the name Mr Chattopadhyay). Coral jumped and scowled at her friend.

"Did you see her hair?" she whispered hoarsely in Nicks's ear.

Mr Chattopadhyay. Mr Chattopadhyay.

"Nicks – seriously – and it just seems to stay up there! Amazing…"

Mr Chattopadhyay. Mr Chattopadhyay.

They came to the fourth door and another reception counter.

"Mr Chattopadhyay, please," burst Nicks with visible relief.

The tall man behind the counter had dark skin and a friendly, dimpled smile. "I am Mr Chattopadhyay."

"And I'm Nicks. This is my friend Coral. And our puppy is called Romeo."

Mr Chattopadhyay leaned across the counter, grinned at Romeo, and then stood back up to his full height.

"Could we have a look at the beach hut ownership records, please?" concluded Nicks.

"Is there a specific beach hut you're interested in?" asked Mr Chattopadhyay.

"That would be Coral Hut," replied Coral with just a hint of self-importance.

Mr Chattopadhyay's dimples deepened. "And which number hut would that be? I don't know each one by name."

Nicks giggled. "Beach hut number five."

Mr Chattopadhyay grinned and winked. "Hold on one moment, please." And then he disappeared behind the tall shelves lined up neatly in rows behind him.

Coral and Nicks waited in patient silence. Romeo sniffed the air and slowly made his way over to the battered coffee bar in the corner. He didn't much like coffee. Sugar was good, in biscuits, and he definitely liked cream. He sniffed the air again.

"I think I have what you're looking for," said Mr Chattopadhyay, who suddenly reappeared from behind the shelves. He spread some documents out along the countertop and began sifting through the papers while he read out loud. "Hut number five – the Promenade, Sunday Harbour… was built in 1908… and bought by Mr Reginald Otter." He glanced up at the girls, who stared back at him expectantly.

It was Coral who finally spoke again. "OK, thanks. But who bought it from Mr Reginald Otter?"

Mr Chattopadhyay smiled and shrugged. "Nobody."

"Nobody?" replied the girls loudly. Even Romeo broke his focus on the cream.

"That's right, nobody. The hut has not been sold since it was built and sold to Mr Reginald

Otter in 1908. It's remained in the same family – probably passed down through the generations, is my guess."

Coral and Nicks digested this new bit of information. And then they thought about the black and white photograph of the two young girls standing, holding hands, on the deck of Coral Hut. Their thoughts settled on the inscription on the photo's cardboard mounting. OUR LOVELY BEACH HUT, it said.

So Mr Reginald Otter must have been Coral's great-great-great-ancestor. But why did Nicks's mum have a photograph of the Hut? And why was it described as 'our lovely beach hut'? Unless... of course...

Coral shook her head vigorously to settle her thoughts. The idea that had just landed in her head was so huge... it was so enormously colossal... that she could not actually speak it out loud just yet.

"Mr Chattopaddy?"

"It's Mr Chattopadhyay," corrected Mr Chattopadhyay.

Coral shrugged apologetically. "Sorry – Mr Chattopadhyay, but how do we find out who the beach hut is registered to? I mean, my aunt passed it down to me and I know my mum got some official papers to prove it. So could we find out who the hut has been passed down to over the years?"

Mr Chattopadhyay nodded. "One moment."

"But that still wouldn't explain why my mum has a photo of Coral Hut that says 'our lovely beach hut'," whispered Nicks urgently.

Coral stared at Nicks, but still could not quite share her new idea with her very best friend yet. It really was an idea of gigantic proportions. Mr Chattopadhyay reappeared to fill the silence.

"We don't hold those records. But you can write away to this address." He slid a beige, oblong compliment slip across the counter to

Coral, who folded it up and slipped it inside her back pocket for safety.

"Thank you very much." Coral turned from Mr Chattopadhyay to face Nicks and Romeo. "Come on, you two, we've got to go."

Nicks was surprised by their sudden hurry and had to run to keep up with Coral, who was taking great strides down the corridor, past the main reception and back out through the main doors.

"Coral, what's the rush?" puffed Nicks when finally they reached the street once again. Romeo, on the other hand, looked like he was just getting warmed up. He licked his nose and bounced about. But Coral was not in a playful mood. She turned to face her best friend with a very intense expression. Her eyes were stretched wide and twinkling. There were blisters of sweat on her top lip, but this had nothing to do with the day's heat.

"Nicks, do you know what this could mean?" she puffed breathlessly.

Nicks's eyes pulled wide as she shook her head slowly, left to right. *Were they due another Einstein moment? Already?*

"Don't you see!" squawked Coral, who was suddenly bubbling over with uncontained excitement. "A long time ago somebody in your family took a photograph of Coral Hut and called it 'our lovely beach hut'. And now we've just discovered that Coral Hut has always remained in my family." Coral paused to let her words take effect. "Nicks, are we... could we be... somehow related?"

in it together

Not a single bit of Nicks moved. She didn't even blink. Even her heart seemed to have stopped its usual steady, reliable beating. She could only stand and stare as Coral's words whizzed around her mind and then slowly began to sink in and make some sense. And even then she couldn't fully grasp their meaning. *Related?*

"Do you think it's possible?" she finally

gasped. Her heart was now suddenly thumping double-time.

Coral paced. "Even if we're just distant relatives... or related by marriage... wouldn't that still be something!"

Nicks nodded in slow motion. "Of course it would. But, well – how can we be sure?"

"Simple." Coral grinned and wrestled the slip of beige paper Mr Chattopadhyay had given her from her back pocket. "We must write away for a list of all the people that Coral Hut has ever been passed down to. And then we should compare that list to your family tree. It's a good place to start anyway. Imagine that, Nicks – not just best friends, but family too. That would be tops!"

Nicks chuckled. "I guess we are rather alike in *some* ways."

"Psht – we're practically identical!" whooped Coral.

"But we shouldn't get too excited just yet," warned the ever-sensible Nicks.

"Mmm," mumbled the eternally dreamy Coral. "But the signs really are all there. Have you noticed just how much we really have in common? I'm talking about things that go way beyond your average, everyday things in common? For example, I love Marmite. And so do you. What are the chances of that? I really don't know anybody else who likes Marmite except for my cousin Archie. And he's family."

Nicks seemed to mull this over, but she remained silent.

"All right then," continued Coral determinedly, "have you ever noticed how we both always put on our left shoes first? And what about how we both like to sleep with the bedroom door open. And we can both wiggle our ears."

Nicks was trying her best to play it cool and calm, but she was getting excited too. Her mouth stretched into a wide, happy grin. And then she remembered her mum's new job. Her smile slipped from its place and pulled down at the corners of her mouth. Saying goodbye to Sunday Harbour and Coral knowing that they were family would make leaving even more difficult – if that were even possible.

"We'll write away for that list of names then," Nicks finally replied with her jaw set firm. "But we've got to concentrate on matchmaking my mum and Mr Sparks first. We mustn't waste a moment."

Coral glanced at her friend. She understood. The Cupid Company's job was now more important than ever. Nothing else mattered as much. They began a slow, thoughtful walk back to Coral Hut.

"It's been weeks since we last saw Mr Sparks," murmured Nicks dully. "I never thought I'd say this, but this really is the worst time for a long summer holiday."

Coral nodded. School was closed and Mr Sparks was off doing who-knew-what. He could be climbing a very distant mountain. Or canoeing through Ecuador. He might be volunteering in Africa. Or scuba diving over the Great Barrier Reef.

"Look – there's Mr Sparks!" cried Nicks suddenly. She pointed and then quickly dropped her hand. What a complete coincidence! Their headteacher was only a short distance away – sniffing the vine tomatoes at Frank's Fruit 'n' Veg.

Coral exhaled. *Wow – it must be a sign! Were they being personally guided by Aphrodite – the goddess of love?* "We have got to say hello," she added conspiratorially as she tightened her grip on Romeo's lead.

"You mean just go over—"

But Coral was already heading boldly in his direction. "Mr Sparks – hello, Mr Sparks!"

The headteacher turned in their direction, still holding a string of plump red vine tomatoes in the air. "Oh, hello, Coral. And hello, Nicola. Are you having a good summer holiday?"

The girls nodded and Romeo yapped three times in a row. A string of bright red balls; he'd never seen such a thing before.

"Are you having a good holiday too, Mr Sparks?" asked Coral. "And how about those tomatoes. Do you enjoy cooking then?"

Mr Sparks seemed to consider this for a moment. "Firstly, I'm not so much on holiday as working considerable hours at the Summer Holiday Club. And these tomatoes are for a soup."

"Would that be soup for one?" wondered Coral just moments before Nicks pinched her elbow.

But Mr Sparks did not appear to be put out by the question. "Actually, it's for a potluck dinner," he replied. "Every guest contributes a dish to the meal. I'm bringing gazpacho."

"Bless you." Coral sniffed.

"Gazpacho is cold tomato soup."

"Italian soup?"

"Spanish soup, actually."

Coral tried not to appear disappointed.

"Anyway, girls, I must be going. I hope you're looking forward to a peaceful and orderly new school term." He stared at Coral for a silent moment.

But the new school term seemed like a lifetime away for both girls. They had far too much to accomplish before then.

"Get better soon," replied Coral.

Nicks waved.

And Mr Sparks wandered off in the direction of Frank's melon section.

"Well, that came to nothing," grumbled Nicks when Mr Sparks had finally disappeared.

Coral shrugged, although Nicks had a point. They needed to achieve something positive today; they couldn't allow themselves to grow disheartened.

"Let's stop at the post office and get that letter sent off," suggested Coral, waving Mr Chattopadhyay's beige slip of paper in the air.

This time it was Nicks who shrugged; she had no better suggestions to offer. So off they went with Romeo lagging behind, sniffing the kerb.

The post office bell tinkled as the trio entered. It was cool and much darker inside and it took their sun-bright eyes a few moments to adjust. Nicks's mum spied them first.

"Hello, girls!" she cried with a smile. "This is a nice surprise."

The post office was empty so they marched right up to the counter.

"Hi, Mrs Waterman, er... Maggie."

"Hi, Mum."

"I hope you're having a good day," said Mrs Waterman, aka Maggie, aka Mum.

Actually it had been a bit of an all-over-the-place sort of day, but neither of the girls really wanted to explain this, so Nicks got straight to the point.

"We need to write a letter, Mum."

"And we need you to post it, please," added Coral.

"Of course – that's what I do." Nicks's mum grinned cheerfully and slid a writing pad and an envelope beneath the post office glass. There were pens attached to silver chains on the countertop.

Nicks quickly scribbled a few sentences, requesting a list of all the people Coral Hut had ever been registered to since it was first built in 1908. Coral, in the meantime, addressed the envelope. And when they were both done, it was Romeo who gave the envelope a lick. They really were a great team.

"There you go, Mum," said Nicks with a very small smile. *What if she and Coral really were related?!* The thought cheered her up. "I'm glad we stopped by," she said to no one in particular.

"Me too," replied her mum, "because I've been meaning to tell you that I'll be going out tomorrow night."

95

"Oh, I don't mind," replied Nicks quickly. "I'll just stay at Coral's house."

"Actually Coral's mum and dad are going out too. We're all going to Mrs Nesbitt's potluck dinner."

"POTLUCK DINNER!" cried both girls at once. The noise startled Romeo, who had dozed off beneath the counter.

Nicks's mum seemed a little alarmed too. "Er, yes, I'll be taking a pasta dish."

"Italian food – of course!" cheered Coral happily.

"I had no idea you were a fan of Italian food, Coral," said Nicks's mum slowly. "Anyway, it should be OK for you both stay at Coral's house. After all, Mrs Nesbitt practically lives across the road."

But neither of the cheerful girls seemed very interested in these minor details. Coral glanced at the heavens and gave Aphrodite a conspiratorial wink.

Feels like Forever

It was the evening of the potluck dinner and Coral's mum checked the lid on the dish of her apple pie. "I'd better leave the ice cream until the last minute," she mumbled to herself as she wiped her hands on her apron.

Coral's father wandered around the kitchen, peering into pots and nosing under anything that wasn't fastened down.

"Have you lost your keys again?" groaned

Coral's mum without even looking up.

"They're not lost... I've just got to find where they are," he replied as he lifted the lid on the dish of apple pie.

"Well, they're not in there! Now, there's the doorbell – I'll find the keys."

Coral's father disappeared and soon reappeared with Nicks, her mum and Coral in tow.

"Doesn't Mrs Waterman look lovely," ooh'd Coral.

Mrs Maggie Waterman did look lovely, but a little uncomfortable. "Erm, thanks, Coral," she stammered as she stroked her glittery chandelier earrings and chiffon summer dress into place. "Nicks insisted... or, uh, helped."

Nicks grinned and patted a stray curl of her mum's hair into place. "Now don't forget an extra squirt of perfume for good luck, Mum."

Coral nodded her agreement. "And it's always a good idea to touch up your lipstick after each course," she advised firmly.

The adults all stared with knotted brows, none of them able to put their confusion into words.

"Look at the time!" said Nicks suddenly. "You'd better all get going. You don't want to make a bad impression by being late."

Coral nodded and patted the pasta dish in Nicks's mum's grip. "And look out for the cold tomato soup. It's not Italian, but still very delicious. YOU WILL LOVE IT!" She winked at Nicks and turned to her own mum. "And don't forget your mobile phone. You know, just in case. We will be home alone, after all."

Nicks's mum especially looked pleased to be leaving; she was the first one to the door. And then they were gone. The almost-empty house seemed very quiet.

"How long do we give them?" wondered Nicks.

"Long enough to get settled, I suppose," replied Coral as she sat down on the sofa and then, feeling restless, quickly shifted over to the piano stool. But she couldn't stay put for long. Pacing in a circle, she tried to imagine what the evening would bring. Would this potluck dinner prove lucky for two desperate best friends?

Nicks kept busy by flicking through the television channels. She then threw treats in the air for Romeo to catch. He grabbed every one with a swift jump and a quick flick of his pink tongue. When they were finally out of treats, Nicks stood and stared out of the window.

"We should call," said Coral, who had finally stopped treading a path in the carpet. She paused with her hand hovering over the cordless telephone. Nicks nodded. So Coral dialled.

"Hi, Mum. Oh yes, everything is just fine. How are you? Oh good. Are you having a good time? Brilliant! And what about Nicks's mum? Uh-mmm. I'm glad she's having a nice time too. So is she talking to anyone in particular? She's talking to everyone, huh? No no, nothing is up. And no, there's nothing much else. OK, then, bye bye now."

Nicks removed her ear from the other side of the earpiece. "They really haven't been there for very long," she commented with a shrug.

"Too right," agreed Coral.

"They've got a long evening ahead."

"Exactly."

"So do we…"

"Mum left us some apple pie?"

"That'll help."

The girls made quick work of two large wedges of hot apple pie with ice cream while Romeo licked daintily at his own blob of ice cream.

"We could make Valentine's cards?" Coral suggested. They always liked to have a ready stock available and she had everything they needed already spread out across the dining table. So the girls settled into two chairs and stared for at least six and a half minutes at the boxes containing felt heart shapes, glitter, sparkles and tiny silver foil cupids.

"Do you think it's too soon to call again?" Coral wondered out loud.

"They're probably sitting down to eat right now," replied Nicks. "I really hope Mr Sparks and Mum are sitting next to each other."

"There's only one way to find out." Coral smiled while she dialled. "Hey, Mum – it's nice to hear from you. Yes, I know I called you. Nope, there's still nothing wrong. I just want to know how you are doing... you know, see if you're having a good time. Good, I'm glad you're trying to. So are you sitting down to eat yet? Oh, that is good; I bet you are hungry. You should try the tomato soup. Mr Sparks made that, you know. And don't worry – it's supposed to be cold, so we don't have to rush. So who are you sitting next to? Other than Dad? Mr Nesbitt? Oh, right. And how about Nicks's mum? Who is she sitting next to?

Wait, Mum – hold on a minute – augh!" Coral stared at the dead phone in her hand and then glanced up at Nicks. "Mum said it was rude to speak on the phone at the dinner table."

"You should probably have got straight to the point then," grumbled Nicks, who was feeling very anxious indeed.

"Don't blame me," growled Coral. "I didn't want to arouse her suspicions by being too blunt."

Nicks sighed. The pressure was definitely getting to them. "Come on, *Snog, Marry, Avoid* is about to start. We need to concentrate on something else."

Coral nodded. *Snog, Marry, Avoid* was one of their favourite television programmes; it was just what they needed. And they almost managed to watch an entire show too. Almost. Coral was fidgeting and tapping the telephone by the third advertising break. By the fourth break she had developed a twitch in her left eye.

"Maybe we should call again?" Nicks finally suggested. "I mean – it has been a while."

Coral didn't need to be told twice.

"Hey, Mu—"

There was a long silence.

"Nope, seriously, Mum, I'm not up to anything," she finally managed. "And no, we haven't broken anything. Yes, Grandma's blue vase is fine. No, Romeo has not pooped on the carpet. I just care about your evening – is that so wrong? I guess we could talk later, but we might be asleep when you get home. And besides, Nicks cares about her mum too and asked me to phone and check if she's OK."

Nicks sat upright and frowned.

"How OK is she exactly? She's been locked in a conversation with Mrs Nesbitt about planting organic vegetables in raised beds, has she? Oh, right. And before that she was talking with Dad about tax credits, was she? Nope, that should be enough information for Nicks. Yes. No, I won't forget to let Romeo out. You're leaving soon? Oh, right. Yes, see you then."

She ended the call and stared glumly at her friend, who stared back like a mirror image. It had been a potluck*less* evening. Perhaps it was the cold tomato soup that had done it. Come to think of it, it was definitely not a romantic sort of starter...

forever young

The sun was already sliding slowly to the other side of the world by the time the girls made their way to the beach the next day. But even though it was late in the afternoon the promenade was still very busy with warm, sun-browned people, happy dogs on leads and seagulls perched and blinking on white wooden railings. The air smelled especially salty and the wind off the ocean was chilled around the edges.

Coral and Nicks didn't speak much as they walked. Romeo was silent too. He was keeping a beady eye on the seagulls; some of them were almost bigger than him. There was a fresh white poster taped to a lamppost. Coral paused and stared at it thoughtfully for a few moments.

"Look at this, Nicks – a poster for the Sea Life Aquarium Open Day. And they're having a Best Beach Finds competition."

Nicks retraced her steps and stood in front of the lamppost. "Oh, right," was all she said.

"All contestants must scour the beach for the best beach find," read Coral. "The winner will receive an ingenious Scientific Weather Forecaster that calculates wind chill and maximum and minimum temperatures as well as being a rain collector. Mmm."

"Or you could just look out of the window," replied an unimpressed Nicks.

"It's a weather *forecaster*, Nicks. Very useful. We should definitely enter."

Nicks shrugged and continued walking. Just that morning she'd overheard her mum on the phone, talking about her possible new job far away. It certainly sounded like she was quite serious too. But Nicks didn't want to tell Coral this.

"Imagine predicting the weather before it happens," continued Coral. "I mean, how brilliant! That would be impressive." She imagined herself standing on the deck of Coral Hut, advising the rest of their beach hut neighbours on the forthcoming weather conditions. Yes, they would all come to her for updates. There would be no more packing something warm *just in case* while she was around.

"Yoo hoo, girls!"

Coral and Nicks glanced up. Meredith was standing on the beach with Malcolm and waving her silver bucket in the air. Romeo yapped and strained at his lead, like he was just in the mood for some more of Malcolm's shortbread.

The girls took the path that cut in between

the glossy red hut and Coral Hut and smiled hellos at their neighbours.

"We're off to collect marine specimens shortly. Would you like to join us?" asked Malcolm. Meredith jiggled her silver bucket in the air just to prove it.

The girls stared thoughtfully.

Perhaps that's just what I need... to think about something else for a bit, considered Nicks.

The ingenious Scientific Weather Forecaster... remembered Coral. *Best beach find here we come!*

"All right then," they both said at once.

Meredith did look pleased. And off they set: two marine scientists, two girls, one silver bucket and a small pup who scowled as they made for the shoreline – further and further away from the shortbread.

"What sort of things are we looking for?" asked Nicks, who was really trying to get involved in the expedition.

Meredith coughed importantly. "We never collect anything that is still alive," she replied seriously. "That is our only rule. Otherwise, we collect anything that is beautiful or interesting or fun. The ocean is wondrous – you never know what you might come across washed up along the shore."

"Collecting useful, valuable or interesting things along the beach is officially called 'beachcombing'," added Malcolm importantly. "I once found a peanut with a shell shaped like a clog. That's a Dutch wooden shoe, by the way."

Meredith chuckled. "We also regularly find things like coloured sea glass, crab shells, exoskeletons of creatures like sea urchins and sea beans, wave-rolled pebbles, shells – oh, heaps of those, and driftwood. We even find things that have been lost or discarded by boats and ships. I once found a bit of pottery printed with HMS WARRIOR. I looked it up – it was crockery from a battleship."

The girls made breathy 'oooh' sounds. "What do you do with your finds?" asked Nicks.

"We're never in one place for very long," admitted Malcolm. "We move around, taking our marine exhibition with us. And all our finds feature in our exhibition. And when we have too many ocean treasures, we return them one by one to the ocean. After all, we're only borrowing…"

Nicks liked this idea very much.

Coral was still thinking about the battleship. A bit of battleship crockery might just win them the ingenious Scientific Weather Forecaster!

The tide had dropped but the tidemark sat high on the soft yellow sand, snaking like a trail along the coastline. Malcolm and Meredith set off in one direction while Coral and Nicks followed the trail in the other. Romeo didn't stray far. Instead he sat and stared out at the ocean with the wind blowing his ears back. He didn't look happy. After all, it was very unlikely that any shortbread had washed ashore.

The sand was gritty and a million different colours close up. There were a lot of shells too, but although they were pretty enough, they weren't particularly special. Nicks knelt down and scooped up the open shell of a mussel covered in pink barnacles. She held it up to show Coral, who nodded in a half-interested sort of way. *That certainly wouldn't win them the ingenious Scientific Weather Forecaster.*

They wandered further along the beach, until Coral found a big lump of sea sponge. She squeezed it and tested it out on her cheek. It did feel lovely, so she kept it tucked inside her palm.

Nicks was next to discover an interesting beach find: the smooth violet shell of a sea snail. She would keep it, she decided, and pass it on to Meredith and Malcolm for their exhibition.

Beachcombing was surprisingly fun. It was

a lot like treasure hunting – although not everything they found was treasure. Coral spied a leaflet sliding across the sand, propelled by the breeze. She trapped it with her foot and made a 'tut tut' sort of sound. She didn't like beach litter. And then she noticed the printing: SUNDAY HARBOUR'S SUMMERTIME OPEN-AIR BEACH CINEMA.

Coral grinned. She'd forgotten all about the open-air beach cinema! For one night of every year all the folks of Sunday Harbour would gather together beneath the stars and enjoy a picnic and a film which was shown on a giant inflatable screen. It was only, like, the best night out ever! She shifted her foot to get a better view of the rest of the writing on the leaflet. It looked like in less than a week they would be sitting on the beach and enjoying a film called *The Love Letter*. This definitely sounded like a romantic film – their favourite! Coral squealed and quickly snapped up the flyer before the wind could carry it away.

"Nicks – look at this!"

Nicks glanced up and frowned. "It's not much of a beach find."

Coral laughed and held the paper out to her friend. "Oh yes it is!"

Nicks read the piece of paper. Then she smiled and nodded. They did love romantic films. And a romantic film beneath the stars was only, like, the most romantic thing ever. Suddenly her head snapped up. Her eyes flew wide and stared into Coral's shiny happy face.

"ARE YOU THINKING WHAT I'M THINKING?" they both cried out.

And suddenly they were both babbling at once.

"Mr Sparks!"

"My mum!"

"It's perfect!"

sista hood

"Strawberries!" declared Coral. "Strawberries dipped in chocolate are very romantic. And what about grapes? Feeding someone grapes is very romantic. I think it goes back to Roman times."

Nicks shook her head to clear it; she really did not want to think too much about Mr Sparks and her mum feeding each other grapes. But it wasn't easy to come up with a list of romantic foods for the beach picnic.

"How about we make a list of first-date foods to avoid instead," she suggested as an alternative to their dead-end thinking. "Like spaghetti – nobody should eat spaghetti on a first date unless they're a gifted spaghetti fork twirler."

Coral nodded. "And garlic is a bad idea – too stinky."

"And chilli with beans." Nicks waved her fingers in front of her nose.

"And sushi."

"Or anything that might get stuck in your teeth. Like spinach is a definite no-no."

"What about a picnic of bite-sized snacks?" suggested Nicks hopefully.

But Coral remained silent so Nicks stared at the pavement while she walked. They really were no closer to finalising the most romantic picnic menu ever as they arrived at Coral's house.

"We should ask your mum," Nicks

suggested, "she's very good at packing picnics."

Pushing open the back door to the kitchen, Coral nearly tripped over as Romeo zigzagged through her legs in the direction of his bowl of food. "What sort of bite-sized snacks?" she mumbled as she tried to remain upright. "Because you do get stinky bite-sized snacks. And ones that get stuck in your teeth."

Nicks shrugged. "I just think that nibbles are always more romantic." Coral's mum happened to be standing in front of the open fridge, surveying its contents.

"Mum, what do you think – are nibbles romantic?" demanded Coral.

Her mum chuckled. "I don't know – you'll have to ask them."

Coral scowled. She never did understand the point of parents trying to be funny. It just wasn't their job. And they were far too old for it anyway. So she ignored her mum's joke.

"OK then – what was the first meal you shared with Dad?" she asked instead.

Coral's mum stared at the ceiling and smiled again. "You know your father – Mr Cheap and Cheerful. I believe we shared a McDonald's drive-through."

Nicks giggled. Coral's mum giggled. Coral shook her head and pushed on regardless. "What food will we be taking along to the beach cinema picnic?" she asked seriously. "Do you think you could pack something special – like romantic foods? After all, they will be showing *The Love Letter*, which will be very romantic... so we... er, might as well continue with the theme." It was the only excuse she could come up with; she really didn't want her mum asking too many questions. After all, her mum was rather friendly with Nicks's mum and the last thing they needed was for her to pass on any ideas.

"Romantic foods..." echoed her mum thoughtfully. "Have you got a boy in mind, Coral?" she asked slyly.

"Oh please, Mother!" *Now she was just getting the wrong idea entirely!*

"I don't mind helping you with a romantic picnic menu, but can't you at least tell me why?" Coral's mum said with a grin.

There was only one way out of this one, decided Coral. She turned slightly and, with her back to Nicks, jabbed a thumb in the direction of her best friend. Coral's mum glanced over to Nicks and then gave a conspiratorial nod.

"You can count on me, girls," she finally replied with a wink. "I'll pack you the best romantic picnic ever. In the meantime, this letter came for you." She held out an official-looking envelope.

The girls turned to each other with eyes as big and round and shiny as hubcaps. *Their reply!* Coral excitedly went to grab the letter, but her mum held it high and waved it in the air.

"What's up?" she wanted to know.

"We're researching the history of Coral Hut, remember?" replied Coral.

Coral's mum nodded – her curiosity satisfied – and released the letter. Coral immediately bounced over to Nicks. She fully expected this to be a monumental moment. "So are you ready for this?" she squealed.

Nicks nodded excitedly. Coral's mum shook her head as she left the kitchen. "You two certainly are extremely excited about finding out the history of a beach hut," she murmured.

Coral tore at the sealed envelope and quickly unfolded two sheets of paper. The first sheet was a polite covering note. The second sheet was an actual list of the names of all the people Coral Hut had ever been passed down to. The girls scanned the names eagerly. Nicks in particular was looking for a name she might recognise as belonging to a member of her own family. But the names meant absolutely nothing to her.

Coral waited patiently without breathing. She was expecting sudden whoops from her best friend. But there still was not a single whoop to be heard.

"Nothing?" she asked nervously.

Nicks shook her head.

"Well, there's only one thing to do, and that's head for your house. We have to compare this list with the names on your family tree."

"Top idea," agreed Nicks.

"See you, Mum – we're off to Nicks's house!"

"Don't be late," came the reply from the next room, but both of the girls were already out of the door. Romeo glanced up, sniffed the air in their wake, and then returned to the gravy biscuits in his bowl. They'd forgotten him in their excitement – not that he minded one bit. Food had made him rather sleepy.

The girls raced up the hill, past the white, wooden garden fences. They flew by the small bakery at the bottom of the road (it still smelled delicious – even at high speeds). Then there was the park, the fruit market with its various striped canopies, more painted houses in rows – this time going downhill – a bus stop and finally Nicks's house.

They arrived breathless, with shiny wet noses and glistening top lips. Thankfully Nicks's mum was not home, so there was no complicated explaining to be done.

Nicks made straight for the large built-in cupboards in her mum's bedroom and removed a folder covered in pressed flowers. Her mum was definitely one for hobbies. Nicks suddenly wondered what hobbies Mr Sparks enjoyed. This was probably something for the Cupid Company to investigate (after all, little information could go a long way).

"Oh, do come on, Nicks!" hissed Coral as her friend seemed to have come to a standstill.

Nicks quickly opened the flowery folder

and extracted a sheet of paper that was covered in lines and scribbled names. The lines were joined like branches. It was her family tree.

Coral unfolded the list of names they'd received in the post and smoothed it out. Then the girls set about comparing the two sheets of paper. Their eyes moved carefully from one list to the other and back again. Coral chewed her lip nervously; Nicks frowned as her eyes darted left then right. They sifted through the names and then started at the top again.

Finally Coral groaned softly. "None of the names tie up!" She slumped on to the double bed. It really was a mystery.

Nicks looked just as disappointed. She'd also desperately been hoping that they would find an answer – that it would turn out they were somehow related. After all, it might just help to convince her mum to stay in Sunday Harbour. She knelt down and retrieved the family photo album and turned to the page with the mounted black and white photograph of the two young girls standing on the deck of Coral Hut. The heart-shaped pendants around the girls' necks shone in the sunlight.

Carefully, she peeled back the protective cellophane sheet and, using her fingernail, gently prised the photograph from the sticky album page. She held it up and stared even closer at the faces of the two young girls for any trace of a nose or a smile she might recognise. After all, everyone was a jigsaw of their relatives. If only the photograph were a close-up...

"Hey – what's that written on the back of the photograph?" asked Coral suddenly.

Nicks flipped the photo over and leaned towards her friend. The writing was curly and the girls read it out loud together.

"*3rd June 1947: For my dearest best friend Betty – I shall never forget you or those*

special summer days we spent at the beach hut. You will be missed so much. Your friend always, Coral." The girls paused.

"BETTY?" cried Nicks.

"CORAL!" shrieked Coral.

"So could this be… is this a photograph of Great-Aunt Coral and her best friend Betty standing on the deck of Coral Hut? And who exactly is Betty?"

"We should check your family tree again," ordered Coral. And they did. They started at the top left and worked their way down the branches.

"There she is!" shouted Nicks excitedly as she jabbed her finger at the name BETTY FITZSIMMONS 1935–2005. She then worked her way backwards, calculating as she went. "It looks… as though… Betty Fitzsimmons was my great-aunt!" she finally announced with a triumphant face – almost like she'd just actually met her great-aunt.

Coral could not believe it. Her voice was

breathy and her eyes glittered. "So your Great-Aunt Betty was very best friends with my Great-Aunt Coral!" she gasped and sighed. *It was almost as good as being related!*

The girls hugged and then stared once again at the writing on the back of the photograph for a few silent moments.

"I wonder what happened to Betty?" Nicks finally said out loud. "Why was your great-aunt going to miss her?"

"Well, she couldn't have died. Look at the dates – Betty lived to be an old lady."

Nicks shrugged uncertainly. She almost didn't want to say the words out loud. "Do you think... uh... did she... move far away from Sunday Harbour?" she finally managed.

Coral stared and then swallowed hard. It would explain why Great-Aunt Coral had said that she would miss her best friend. It would also explain why Nicks hadn't known her great-aunt. Maybe Betty really had moved very far away. The girls stared at the photograph – at the matching shiny, heart-shaped pendants that hung from the girls' necks. These were quite obviously friendship pendants. And then Nicks flipped the photograph over again. They stared at the date on the back: 3rd June 1947. Betty would have been twelve years old. Great-Aunt Coral too. They were exactly the same age then as Coral and Nicks were now. Could fate be cruel enough to repeat the past?

beach chums

Was it possible to fly sky high with happiness but still feel restless and anxious at the same time? That was precisely how the girls felt. Their great-aunts had been very best friends once upon a time – a long time ago – which meant that being best friends was in their genes. Coral and Nicks were actually destined to be best friends – and you couldn't be better friends than that!

They might as well have been related. But what if Nicks had to leave Sunday Harbour? It seemed too heart-wrenching to contemplate.

Coral was standing in the middle of Coral Hut with her hands on her hips. You couldn't find a more romantic place. Not only was it the Cupid Company headquarters, but it was also filled with soft, pretty colours, fragrant flowers and chubby cherubs – a shrine to love!

"If only we could transport Coral Hut to the beach cinema picnic," murmured Coral, more to herself than anything. But Nicks heard every word.

"We could try our best," she replied with a smile. She was just as determined to remain positive. "Look here – we'll use this pretty woollen throw as a picnic blanket. And there are scented candles inside the white wicker basket. We'll take some of these scatter cushions along. And this enamel flower jug filled with roses is perfect for the centre of the blanket."

Coral grinned at her very smart best friend. Her mum was arranging a menu of romantic foods. And now they had a beautiful beach picnic organised. Everything was coming together. But they only had one more day to make their final plans for the big event. And everything needed to be timed to perfection. Coral thought about James Bond and the movies she had watched, sometimes over and over (they were a perfect combination of mystery and love).

"We should call the beach picnic 'Operation Spark of Love'," she declared boldly with her finger raised in the air.

But Nicks did not seem particularly impressed. She did not appreciate Mr Bond quite as much as her best friend.

At that moment, Romeo started barking and the girls glanced up to find Meredith and

Malcolm heading towards them. Malcolm was carrying a strange-looking device that appeared to be a pole with a small flying saucer attached to the end.

"Hey, girls!" he called out eagerly. He did seem very excited about something. "Look what we have here."

"It's a metal detector!" cried Meredith.

"Which is a device that uses electromagnetic induction to detect metal that is buried," explained Malcolm. "Its uses include the detection of land mines or the finding of hidden weapons – like at airports. It can also be used for archaeology. But best of all – it's exactly what you need if you're a beachcomber hunting for very special treasure."

Much of Malcolm's first sentence was lost on the girls, but they certainly got the treasure-hunting part. Clambering down Coral Hut's striped steps, they joined their neighbours on the beach. Malcolm demonstrated the detector's on-off switch and explained how they would hear a beeping sound when the machine came across metal. All they had to do was sweep the detector left then right, just above the surface of the sand.

"What sort of treasures could we find?" wondered Coral, who was quite certain that beachy things like shells and driftwood did not contain metal.

"There are heaps of treasures to be found in the sand," cried Malcolm. "Navy buttons and brooches. Shipwreck artefacts like old coins and spoons. Rings and watches. Horseshoes and even cannonballs! You could join a metal-detecting club if you really enjoy treasure hunting."

Coral thought about this. She was less interested in joining a club. But a cannonball – now that would surely win them the Best Beach Finds competition! She could almost feel the smooth weight of the ingenious

Scientific Weather Forecaster resting heavily in the palm of her hand.

"Do you think we could we have a go with the detector?" she asked.

"Sure, it's yours for an hour," agreed Malcolm. "Unfortunately it doesn't belong to me, so I will need it back. Have fun!"

The girls set off, with Romeo bouncing alongside the metal detector, barking and trying to bite its pole. They would never find any treasure with his help! So Nicks scooped him up in her arms while Coral swept the flying saucer this way and that, listening carefully for the tell-tale beep-beep sound.

The girls continued on in this way for at least fifteen metres without hearing so much as a single beep. Coral's shoulders were beginning to droop with the combined weight of the detector and her growing disappointment when all of a sudden the machine blared out a shrill beep-beep, beep-beep sound. They jumped and then grinned, although Coral was very careful to make sure that she did not jiggle the metal detector around too much. She kept an eye and ear trained on the precise spot in the sand and knelt slowly down. And then she got busy digging a hole faster than she'd ever dug before. Romeo immediately lent a paw, and before long, there was yellow beach sand flying and a hole growing deeper in the ground. And then Coral's fingers closed on something hard and cold.

"I have something!" she announced.

"What is it?" cried Nicks excitedly.

Coral held her breath, lifted their beach find into the air… and groaned. It was just a small tin can – quite possibly the worst beach find ever.

"Let me have a go," said Nicks. And so off they went once more, although this time Romeo ran alongside the metal detector without barking or biting it once. He was good at quickly getting used to new things.

Instead of walking a straight line, Nicks chose to arc in a half-moon shape – up the beach and down to the shoreline once again. For a while there was nothing. And then came that wonderfully exciting beep-beep sound once again.

"Stop!" squealed Coral happily. Instantly, they fell to their knees and using their cupped hands like spades, started digging once more. This time it was Nicks who felt the metal treasure first. It was a copper key – the sort that might fit a padlock. It was not really an interesting sort of key.

"Mmff," grumbled Coral, who had been expecting very great things. She was now beginning to doubt this business of metal detecting. At least shells were nice to look at.

"Come on, let's give it one more go," urged Nicks. "Malcolm did say we could keep it for an hour."

Coral stood still and contemplated the suggestion. She'd always been a positive sort of girl. It really wasn't in her to give up. And besides, wasn't it *third time lucky*? There was a good chance that their fortune was about to change. So she picked up the metal detector and held it out firmly in front of her.

"Yes – let's go for it!" she finally replied. It felt like Aphrodite, the goddess of love, was spurring her on.

It didn't take very long for the beep-beep sound to be heard again. But the girls were much slower to fall to their knees this time. They were calmer and more thoughtful about digging for this treasure. Perhaps this was simply what becoming experienced treasure hunters was all about.

It was Coral who first felt something other than the sand. She let her fingers slither slowly over this new treasure's cold, hard shape before gripping its end and pulling it firmly from the sand. And then she stared at it long and hard. It was a metal L-shape and had probably once been attached to something else. Maybe it had been part of a hinge or bracket of some sort, but on its own – today it was simply an L-shape.

"You know what this is, don't you?" Coral said to her friend with a serious sense of importance.

Nicks shook her head slowly. "Nope, I'm afraid I really don't," she replied (although she wished she did).

"It's a sign!" announced Coral. "Well... actually... it's an L-shape. But an L-shape is a sign. It's a good-luck sign."

Poor Nicks looked more confused than ever.

So Coral explained. "This is an L-shape, right? And L is a letter, right?" Nicks nodded. "And the movie showing at the open-air beach cinema is called *The Love Letter*. The word love starts with L. And L is a letter. So you see, this letter L," concluded Coral, the L-shape now held victoriously in the air, "means that the picnic date is going to be a huge success!"

Nicks blinked a few times and nodded thoughtfully. *A hinge (or bracket) would not have been quite as symbolic, that was for sure.*

could this be forever?

It was the evening of the open-air beach cinema and a bright half-moon hung high in the sky. The sea breeze had tired itself out, leaving the outside air warm and calm. The ocean had grown sleepy too and lapped gently at the hard, cooling sand. The perfect evening for a romantic picnic.

The girls had their plan carefully worked out too. Nicks had already left for her house (after all, somebody had to make sure that her mum dressed for love), while Coral remained at the beach hut. She'd already filled her heart-shaped backpack with scented candles and flowers and her arms were wrapped tightly around the pretty printed scatter cushions and soft woollen blanket. She patted the binoculars slung across her shoulders. *Check.* She tapped the whistle around her neck. *Check.* And then she consulted her watch; it was now time to leave.

The picnic area was only a short distance away and Coral was one of the first to arrive, which was just how they'd planned it. Choosing a prime spot that was close (but not too close) to the temporary giant inflatable cinema screen, Coral checked her watch again. It was exactly oh-seven-seventeen-p.m. She hoped that Nicks was keeping a firm eye on her own watch too. They had a strict schedule to keep, but she could not forget that her best friend really did not get the whole 'secret agents of love' thing like she did.

Finally Coral's parents arrived, carrying a large picnic basket between them.

"Are you actually lifting at all?" complained Coral's father loudly.

"Course I am," snapped Coral's mum with a grin and a wink.

Coral watched her parents and checked her watch once again. It was oh-seven-twenty-seven-p.m.

"You are late!" she cried out.

As an accountant Coral's father considered himself a man of numbers, and he checked his own watch before nodding irritably and muttering something about 'seven minutes – the time it takes your mum to apply her lipstick'.

Actually, Coral was a little behind schedule too, but she kept this to herself, hurriedly unpacking the candles and flowers and scattering the cushions carefully across the woollen blanket.

Coral's mum spread their trusty old tartan family picnic blanket right beside the pretty woollen one. She then started unpacking food from the basket, introducing each dish as she did so.

"Vegetable sticks with hummus dip," she began.

Coral didn't move. *Veg 'n' dip – yawn!*

"Chicken liver pate."

There was never a good time for liver.

"Fresh strawberries with dipping chocolate."

"Oh, brilliant!" cheered Coral, quickly scooping up the strawberries and chocolate before moving them from the tartan blanket to the pretty woollen one.

Of course Coral's mum noticed. She paused and blinked, but did not comment. "Barbecue-chicken drumsticks," she said instead.

Coral didn't budge. *Drumsticks – too caveman.*

"Cucumber sandwiches."

Coral eyed the sandwiches. They were heart-shaped. Clever mum with her cookie cutter! She made a grab for the sandwiches.

"Crisps."

Coral read from the packet – *cheese and onion* – and quickly passed.

"Prawn kebabs."

Coral thought about this. Seafood was a bit special. So she quickly claimed those too.

"Gruyère cheese straws."

She frowned. *Super stinky!*

"Fruit cake."

Coral smiled as she quickly claimed the cake and delivered it to the blanket.

"Homemade fudge."

Coral claimed that too.

"Are we having separate picnics, Coral?" her mum finally asked.

"Er, sort of. So what else do you have in there?"

"Why don't you unpack the rest of the basket," her mum replied. "You seem to have your own ideas about everything." And with that, she wandered off to speak with Mrs Nesbitt, who had just arrived.

So Coral did, and very soon the food on the blanket was joined by a pack of berry biscuits, a bunch of fresh grapes, a bag of sugared almonds and a bottle of sparkly pink drink. She smiled and checked her watch. Operation Spark of Love was well underway. And Nicks and her mum were due to arrive at any moment.

They arrived at precisely oh-seven-thirty-nine-p.m., which was not very precise at all.

"You're nine minutes late," hissed Coral at her best friend. And then she smiled at Maggie Waterman, who did not seem very smiley at all. But she did look like she was dressed for love. At least Nicks had got that right. "Your mum looks perfect," she added in a whisper.

Nicks frowned and harrumphed. "Well, she doesn't think so – she didn't want to wear any of it!" she grumbled hoarsely.

But Coral was too busy admiring Maggie Waterman's Valentine's-inspired outfit. It was bright and beautiful and very romantic. You couldn't miss her bright red dangly heart earrings and matching wide belt. Her white dress was pretty too and accessorised with a heart-shaped brooch that complemented the small red shiny hearts the girls had glued to the toes of her shoes.

Maggie Waterman noticed Coral's mum and quickly sidled up close to her. "I thought this was meant to be a themed evening!" she groaned out loud as she pointed to Coral's mum's plain denim jeans and blouse. She then glanced around at the rest of the picnickers and groaned out loud once more. Nobody else had dressed up either!

Coral figured that this could only work to their advantage; Mr Sparks certainly could not overlook Maggie Waterman now. But Maggie Waterman did not look happy and now she was looking for Nicks.

Quickly, Coral consulted her watch. It was almost oh-seven-forty-five-p.m. She patted the binoculars hanging around her neck and checked that Nicks was wearing hers too. The girls knew that Mr Sparks was never early, but it was getting late – he wouldn't be long now.

Splitting up, they watched and waited for their headteacher's arrival. Nicks spied him first through her binoculars and raced over to him, blowing sharply into her whistle as she ran. Mr Sparks looked surprised and quite startled.

"Good evening, Mr Sparks. This way, please," she announced and then, noticing his confused expression, quickly added, "It is allocated seating!"

Mr Sparks scratched his head and followed his student. Coral, meanwhile, had clearly heard Nicks's whistle and immediately hightailed it back to the picnic area.

"I think they're almost ready to start the film," she announced to the parents mingling nearby. "We'd better sit down – *now!*"

The adults looked a little perplexed, but left their conversations hanging mid-air and went to sit down.

"Not there!" yelled Coral at Maggie Waterman, whose bottom had almost landed on the tartan picnic blanket.

Maggie Waterman jumped up and looked vaguely terrified. Her big dangly red heart earrings were jangling up and down.

"You, uh… need to sit here, please," added Coral with forced calm. She pointed sternly at the pretty woollen blanket.

Coral's mum had been watching carefully and she shrugged and made a move to join Maggie Waterman. "Not you!" cried Coral, whose nerves were feeling quite ragged by now. Everyone was looking at her quite strangely and there was still no sign of Mr Sparks or Nicks. And then – like the sun appearing from behind a cloud – they suddenly emerged through the crowd. "Oh look!" cried Coral with visible relief. "Mr Sparks – what a brilliant surprise! You must come and *SIT RIGHT HERE*."

Mr Sparks smiled politely at the parents and nodded nervously. "I had no idea it was allocated seating," he mumbled as he sat down on the blanket beside Maggie Waterman, the romantic food, candles, flowers and scatter cushions.

"Hello, Maggie," he said, "you have put on a lovely spread."

But there was no time for Maggie Waterman to explain.

"I've bought some of my own delicious dishes too," continued Mr Sparks as he reached for his small cooler box. "Homemade chilli chips, garlic pork ribs and ginger beer!"

Coral groaned.

Maggie shifted on the blanket to make room for the chips, ribs and ginger beer. Mr Sparks immediately noticed her shoes with the red shiny hearts. Maggie noticed him noticing and blushed as red as the glued-on hearts.

"Erm, I thought it was a themed evening," she stammered, quickly hiding the shoes beneath the hem of her dress.

"The movie is called *The Love Letter* and it's very romantic," explained Coral as she settled herself down on the tartan picnic blanket beside her parents. "Come on, Nicks!" She patted the two-centimetre-square bit of unclaimed tartan picnic blanket still remaining.

Coral's mum's gaze moved from their crowded picnic blanket to the blanket that was currently home to only two. She then raised her eyebrows and rolled her eyes as if to say, *What is Coral up to now?*

But it was too late for her to say anything. The movie had started and the crowd were settled, focusing on getting to grips with its characters and story – everyone except for Coral and Nicks, that was.

By leaning backwards and as far left as she could manage without toppling over, Coral had managed to carefully slide the Tupperware of garlic pork ribs from under Mr Sparks's nose and in the direction of the picnickers behind them. She turned and smiled and nodded at their fellow foodies so that they would know that the ribs were a gift.

Nicks, meanwhile, set about subtly scenting the air with a few puffs of French rose air freshener which she had got camouflaged under a cotton hat.

Suddenly Mr Sparks started sneezing. Over and over. And it wasn't just a short burst of a polite sneeze either. The man sounded like a ship coming in. Maggie Waterman stared.

So Coral quickly distracted her with a tube of raspberry glitter lip gloss. It would look very lovely in the candlelight.

Maggie Waterman looked confused as her daughter's best friend unexpectedly passed her the make-up. She stared at the tube and then stared suspiciously back at Coral before handing the lip gloss back again, unopened.

But Coral couldn't let Maggie Waterman become suspicious, so she quickly passed the gloss on to her mum, who happily applied a thick coating. Coral's father frowned at his wife, who now glinted in the moonlight. He then rolled his eyes at the night sky, as if her glittery lips might just land a spaceship.

Mr Sparks had finally stopped sneezing and was feeling around for his garlic pork ribs. He felt Maggie Waterman's knee instead.

Both girls sat instantly taller. *Finally, some progress!*

"Oh, pardon me," he whispered awkwardly, quickly running his hand through his hair, quite obviously at a loss.

The light from the moon above was suddenly blocked out by two tall, looming shapes. The girls glanced up to find Meredith and Malcolm standing over them, grinning sheepishly.

"We're a bit late," whispered Meredith, "would you mind if we joined your picnic?"

Coral and Nicks stared at each other in horror. Of course they knew exactly what would happen next.

"Of course not," replied Coral's mum. "There's plenty of room on the other blanket."

The girls groaned in unison. But if Mr Sparks or Maggie Waterman were put out, they hid it well. Hurriedly, they shifted backwards. Maggie Waterman sat in the homemade fudge along the way, while Mr Sparks succeeded in knocking over the dipping chocolate. Not that he noticed.

152

"What a pretty picnic!" cooed Meredith as she settled on to a gingham scatter cushion in between Mr Sparks and Maggie Waterman. She admired the enamel jug of flowers and smiled. "It's rather romantic – if you're... uh... into that sort of thing."

Malcolm bobbed his head up and down in agreement. "And I think they're showing a romantic comedy. So you could say that love is in the air," he added with a slight stammer, like he was not used to talking about love.

"Do have some fruit cake," Maggie Waterman smiled and offered politely.

"How about a chilli chip?" added Mr Sparks.

And then everyone fell silent, they were all so busy munching and watching the movie.

But Coral and Nicks had long since given up on the movie. They'd pretty much given up on the romantic picnic too. They simply sat and stared, feeling overwhelmed by a sense of glumness.

And then Malcolm leaned towards Meredith. "Would you like a strawberry dipped in chocolate?" he asked his research partner in a whisper. She shrugged and nodded. So with a slightly trembling hand he fed her the chocolate end of a strawberry. She giggled. He giggled. And then they returned to watching the movie.

Coral sighed and also stared back at the movie while she listened to Mr Sparks chewing on his chilli chips.

A few more moments passed and then this time it was Meredith who leaned forward. "These prawn kebabs are a treat – here, try one, Malcy," she whispered.

Malcy? Coral's head turned quickly. But Malcy was already munching on a prawn with a large satisfied smile.

And then they all returned to watching the movie again. But not for long.

The peaceful evening air suddenly shattered with the sound of a loud gasp quickly followed by a sharp and very piercing scream.

"SNAAKKKEEE!!"

Every nearby head turned in panic. *Snake?*

There were startled cries as terrified picnickers jumped to their feet – but nobody quicker than Maggie Waterman.

"THERE IS A SNAKE ON OUR BLANKET!" she screamed once more.

The ever-optimistic Coral still had not given up on the evening entirely, and she suddenly wondered if Mr Sparks might just single-handedly catch the snake and save Maggie Waterman... and win her heart forever.

"SNAKE?! ON THE BLANKET?!" shrieked Mr Sparks as he jumped to his feet and did a graceless Irish jig.

Even Coral's father had backed away from their picnic. Nobody seemed to keep a calm head – except for Coral. She turned away from the chaos of jigging and screaming and stared

153

thoughtfully at the picnic blanket. There was a snake, it was true – a very dark, very brown snake, that stretched all the way over to the overturned bowl of dipping chocolate.

Someone knocked over the enamel jug of flowers, sending the water flowing like a river to meet the snake, which, Coral now noted with a sigh of relief, was a chocolate snake – the very chocolate dip that Mr Sparks had knocked over when he'd gone to make more room on the blanket. And then, one by one, everyone seemed to take notice and laugh. Before long there were more screams of hilarity than fear.

Maggie Waterman stood by and giggled in her Valentine's-inspired outfit.

Coral's mum hooted with the ridiculousness of it all.

Mr Sparks became distracted by a Tupperware of garlic pork ribs he'd noticed sitting on the blanket of their neighbouring picnickers.

Coral's father tapped his watch and wondered if the organisers would consider rewinding the last five minutes of the movie he'd missed so that he got his full money's worth.

And Malcolm bent low and picked up one of the roses that had fallen out of the overturned enamel jug. He stood upright and presented the rose to Meredith, who smiled shyly but seemed to glow.

Coral and Nicks turned to each other and shrugged. *Had Cupid's arrow landed just a little left of its target?*

school mates

The laughs created by the chocolate snake had put everyone in a good mood, and after the film nobody was in much of a hurry to leave for home. The inhabitants of Sunday Harbour seemed happier than ever to stand amongst the picnic debris, nattering and nibbling leftovers and having fun together. Maggie Waterman looked just like everyone else again – now that she'd removed the dangly red

earrings, matching wide belt and her shoes
with hearts.

Meredith and Malcolm seemed especially
chatty. Or perhaps, as the newest additions to
Sunday Harbour, they simply still had the
most to talk about. Everyone else knew each
other quite well already.

"So that's why we're here," concluded
Meredith with a satisfied sigh. "We have made
it our mission to see the starfish renamed as
the sea star – because the starfish is simply
not a fish."

Mr Sparks listened closely and tapped his
chin thoughtfully. It was clear that a teacher's
mind was always open to facts and new
information.

Coral's mum nodded briskly to show that
she really did love a good campaign. Coral's
father stared at his feet. He quite clearly did
not get the whole fish-star thing. Maggie
Waterman's mind seemed to be elsewhere
too. Nicks knew her mum better than

anybody; was she thinking about the new job far away?

But the pair of marine scientists were not finished talking about their cause just yet. Malcolm quickly picked up from where Meredith had left off.

"Unfortunately," he continued, "our sea star campaign is not progressing as well as we'd hoped. We're trying to get a petition going, but it's not proving easy. You see, we haven't received a huge amount of local interest."

"You need posters!" declared Mr Sparks suddenly, his finger raised in the air. "That's your problem – nobody knows what you're up to."

Malcolm considered this for a moment. And then he nodded. "Yes, I suppose you're right. But we don't have an advertising budget."

"What about the Summer Holiday Club?" suggested Coral's mum. "Mr Sparks, you're always telling us what an artistic bunch the children are."

The headteacher thought about this for a moment. "Mmm, true. They are very creative. But that sort of project takes a great deal of coordinating. And we're very short staffed. Most of our teachers are away on holiday."

Coral's spine snapped straight. She blinked, breathed deep and jabbed an elbow in her best friend's side. Nicks yelped, but she needed no further prompting.

"Mum – you're a teacher!" she cried out.

Maggie Waterman was startled by the announcement. Everyone stared at her, some in surprise.

"Maggie – you're a teacher?"

Maggie Waterman coughed nervously. "I was – a long time ago."

Just then Nicks remembered the folder of pressed flowers her mum had made by hand. "Mum, you're so creative too," she added proudly.

Her mum smiled. She laughed at her daughter, and then nodded. "Thank you, Nicks. And I suppose I'd be happy to help in any way I can."

"In that case, I'm quite sure that the Holiday Club can oblige with a few colourful sea star posters," replied Mr Sparks. He remained silent for a few thoughtful moments before continuing. "Come to think of it, the Sea Life Aquarium Open Day is coming up – it's the ideal time to collect petition signatures. Just about everyone will be there."

Meredith and Malcolm turned to each other and grinned. "Of course!" they cried in unison. "It's the perfect time and place."

"And we'd be happy to help collect petition signatures!" added Coral's mum excitedly.

"We shall have to include all this information on the posters," instructed Mr Sparks – with a smile directed straight at Maggie Waterman, Coral noted. "It's a very good cause. After all, the starfish is not a fish. And that's a fact."

Meredith smiled gratefully. "It's a great idea. We've been so busy helping to organise the Aquarium Open Day we didn't even consider how it might benefit our sea star campaign."

"You really must let me help," said Coral's mum, who was one of Sunday Harbour's top volunteers.

"You should come along and meet the aquarium's new manager," replied Meredith. "He's the man in charge. The Best Beach Finds competition was his very own idea."

Coral's mum listened and nodded. "That's what I'll do then," she agreed. Heads turned towards each other and then everyone cheered.

"Here's to the sea star!"

"And the Aquarium Open Day."

"And to chocolate snakes!"

163

This particular 'here's to' made everyone chuckle. Even Coral's father nodded enthusiastically (and nobody had mentioned maths or massive discounts at all). It was just like the folks of Sunday Harbour to come together over something. But Coral's grin really was the widest grin of them all. Of course she realised that there really was not much time left to find the best beach find if she wanted to win the ingenious Scientific Weather Forecaster. And naturally she cared about the little sea stars and the Aquarium Open Day too, but at that moment there was only one thing she could think about: *Maggie Waterman and Mr Sparks were now bound by a cause!* And that meant that the girls now stood the best chance ever of getting them to fall in love.

Coral thought once more about Great-Aunt Coral and her best friend Betty. She imagined the two young girls standing on the deck of Coral Hut, holding hands, with their heart-shaped lockets glinting in the sunlight. And then she turned to Nicks and smiled. Perhaps these two best friends wouldn't be separated after all.

PUPPY PALS

The beach at Sunday Harbour was never short of children running and digging and playing tag with the waves, and the following day was no different. There were also people lounging in canvas beach chairs and leafing through newspapers. There were ladies in hats and big sunglasses eating frozen yoghurt on sticks. There were dog walkers. There were beachcombers.

And then there were beachcombers with dogs.

"Hey, look there," said Coral from her place on the deck of Coral Hut. "Metal detectives!"

Nicks followed her friend's outstretched arm. Sure enough, walking along the beach up ahead were three men and one woman, each with a metal detector, scanning the sand for treasures.

"I'd love to have another go at being a metal detective," added Coral wistfully. There was not a huge amount of difference between being a secret agent and a detective, and she thought she might have a talent. But more importantly, she had an ingenious Scientific Weather Forecaster to win. She clasped her hands tightly together and sighed happily. Now that they had a new plan in place she felt confident that Maggie Waterman would soon forget all about moving far away. For today the girls did not have urgent plans to hatch or problems to solve. Now all they had to do was simply sit and wait and watch.

And watch they did – Meredith and Malcolm strolling along the beach in the direction of their rented red beach hut. They didn't seem to be in any particular hurry either, and walked close enough for their shoulders to touch. Meredith was busy peeling an orange and she offered Malcolm half of the fruit when she was done. He smiled his thanks and then tucked a loose curl of her hair behind her ear. She giggled. He blushed.

The girls watched without speaking. Things certainly seemed to have changed between the two research partners. It appeared as though researching was now the very last thing on their minds. Romance had clearly taken over. Nicks grinned. As did Coral. Of course it was they themselves who'd had everything to do with this recent romantic turn of events!

The strolling pair waved as they mounted

the steps to their beach hut. The girls waved back, although Coral still kept one interested eye trained on the metal detectives.

"Do you think we could borrow your metal detector again?" she called out to their neighbours.

Meredith paused her delicate giggling and leaned over the deck railings. "Sorry, Coral," she replied, "but we don't have it right now. I think I might have mentioned that it doesn't actually belong to us. But certainly when we get the metal detector again, then of course you can have another go with it."

Coral gave this some thought as she gazed out at the four metal detectives sweeping the beach. Her gaze narrowed. It wasn't the answer she'd been hoping for – after all, she didn't have very much time left. Wistfully, she looked out to sea, hoping that they wouldn't find all the beach treasure before her.

"Now come on, girls, this shouldn't stop you from treasure hunting!" cried Malcolm excitedly. "There's always the old-fashioned way." He smiled and held out the silver metal bucket.

The old-fashioned way was better than no way, so the girls agreed. Setting off with Romeo, who carried the silver bucket in his mouth, they headed up the beach and away from the metal detectives. They didn't speak much; they were both too busy with the thoughts in their heads.

Coral was thinking about winning the Best Beach Finds competition and the ingenious Scientific Weather Forecaster. *Come to think of it, if she won the forecaster but didn't tell people that she had, they might think that she had developed mysterious predicting powers...*

Meanwhile Nicks was wondering about the Summer Holiday Club – and her mum and the headteacher. *It was up to the adults now, but would sparks fly between them? She hoped he would live up to his name...*

"Maybe we should offer our help?" she suddenly suggested out loud. "That way we can keep a close eye on them."

Coral stooped to pick up a piece of driftwood, which looked a lot like a piece of hull from an old Roman shipwreck. "To help with what? And who should we keep a close eye on?" she replied distractedly.

"At the Holiday Club. Mr Sparks and my mum."

Coral shrugged. Of course she saw what Nicks was getting at. It wasn't a half-bad idea either.

Romeo dropped the silver bucket and picked up a dark brown heart-shaped pod-type thing instead. He nudged Coral's leg with it. She looked at it closely. *Oooh, a heart shape.* She plopped it inside the bucket and patted Romeo's head.

They had only walked a bit further when Coral suddenly fell on all fours to inspect the sand closely. "Look at this!" she cried out. "It must be a shark's tooth." She held what looked like a white jagged piece of stone for her fellow treasure hunters to examine. Romeo sniffed her palm disinterestedly and then sniffed the sand instead.

Nicks shrugged noncommittally. "I guess it could be."

"Well, if it's not a shark's tooth, then it's some other sea creature's tooth," said Coral, "which is still interesting." *But would it win her the Scientific Weather Forecaster?*

Romeo stopped his sand sniffing and came to a sudden stop with his four legs spread wide. He stretched his neck so that he looked taller and his small ears pricked forward. His deep brown eyes were locked in on something. He stared, still and silent. Only his nose twitched as he smelled the air. A sudden sea breeze whipped up his coat, ruffling the fur on his little body. But still Romeo did not budge an inch. He seemed positively mesmerised.

Coral and Nicks stopped walking too. They stared at the motionless pup. And then they followed his rigid gaze. He appeared to be focused on a very furry, rather round dog playing catch with its owner just a short distance away.

A high-pitched whimper escaped from Romeo's little doggy lips. And then he shivered.

"Are you all right, boy?" asked Coral as she bent down on one knee.

But still Romeo stared, unmoving.

"I don't think I've ever seen that other dog before," said Nicks as she studied the furry, off-white pup from a distance.

Suddenly Romeo gave a single short, sharp bark. And then he was gone – racing down the beach faster than a bat in a blizzard.

"Romeo!" cried Coral.

But it looked as though Romeo would stop at nothing, well – except possibly for a short, fat off-white pup. He almost crashed right into the other dog.

"Romeo, come here!"

But even if Coral's words hadn't been carried away on the sea breeze they would probably have proved useless anyway. As Romeo stood there, sniffing the other dog, it looked like he'd forgotten all about the rest of the world around him.

Coral stared ahead nervously. She had never ever known Romeo to fight, but she still couldn't help worrying. *Could she get to him in time?*

Suddenly Romeo stopped sniffing the other dog, who still hadn't moved a muscle. He opened his doggy jaws wide. His long pink tongue came rolling out. And then he gave the other pup an almighty lick right across the nose. He seemed to be grinning as he tilted his face to the blue sky and let out a long, heartfelt howl. He was – quite clearly – in love.

friends in need

"Is that your dog?" said the man with the fat, furry pup.

Coral and Nicks had been so focused on the dogs that until now they hadn't done much more than glance at the new dog's owner. The man was very tall, with broad shoulders and long legs like a runner. He had dark hair and wide, kind eyes. He smiled at the girls while he waited for their reply. His teeth were very white and very straight.

"Yes, that's my dog," confirmed Coral. "His name is Romeo."

"He is lovely," said the man as he tapped Romeo's love-struck head.

Coral laughed out loud. "And I think he likes your dog very much."

The man smiled lovingly at his pup. "This is Miss Honey," he said.

"She certainly is a honey," chuckled Nicks as she tickled the dog's slightly mucky chin.

Romeo gave Miss Honey another lick and nuzzled close to her. As experts in the field of love, the girls of course knew about love at first sight, but this was the first time they'd actually seen it in action.

"What have you been collecting?" asked the tall man, peering forward nosily.

Nicks showed him the contents of their bucket.

"We're beachcombing!" she said, just as Coral exclaimed, "We're treasure hunting!"

The man inspected their treasure and made

a 'mmm' sound. "This," he finally said as he picked up the dark brown heart-shaped pod in his hand, "is a sea bean. And that's a rather nice piece of driftwood you have there."

"Do you think it might be part of a Roman shipwreck?" asked Coral.

The man laughed loudly, showing all his white teeth. "I know a bit about marine life, but I'm no archaeologist. Although I do think that your Roman shipwreck theory is probably unlikely. " He chuckled some more, which made Coral feel a teeny bit silly. Nicks seemed to find it very funny though.

"Well, did you know that the starfish is really a sea star, because it's not even a fish at all?" demanded a slightly flustered Coral.

"That's absolutely true," agreed the man.

"Oh, right," mumbled Coral, who had been counting on the man *not* knowing about the starfish. She stared down at Romeo, who seemed to have found a gift for Miss Honey in the sand. He picked it up in his mouth and offered it to the object of his affection. But Miss Honey just turned away.

"Poor pup," murmured Coral as she prised the unwanted gift from Romeo's jaws. Being in the business of matchmaking meant that she knew how love worked; she'd seen it go wrong many times before.

In her hand she now held what looked like a black pincushion with fine curly tendrils growing from each corner. She turned it this way and that, examining each angle, trying to imagine what it might be.

"Oh, look at that!" said the man, the moment he noticed the beach find in Coral's hand. "It's a mermaid's purse."

"A mermaid's purse!" cried Coral, who had always secretly believed in extraordinary things like unicorns, fairies and mermaids.

The man smiled. "Astonishing, isn't it?" he agreed.

Nicks grimaced and frowned. "Mermaid?"

"I always knew it!" added Coral excitedly.

"A mermaid's purse is actually the name for a shark's egg case. But it is still a rather unusual beach find – well done, Romeo," said the man.

Coral was only mildly disappointed (after all – a shark's egg case did not mean that mermaids didn't actually exist... or have purses... and other really useful fashion accessories...). And besides, according to this man, it was apparently quite an unusual beach find. *But was it more unusual than a shark's tooth?* She fished the tooth out of the silver bucket and boldly handed it over to the man. "So what do you think of this?"

He accepted the tooth and inspected it seriously. "It's OK – for a small, eroded seashell."

"An eroded seashell!" Coral scowled.

"This little shell has no doubt been dragged along the seabed and dumped on the shore by the currents – and that's why it's this unusual shape. It's a good enough beach find too." He grinned happily, like a good beach find was exactly what life was really about. "My name is Ben, by the way. Now we really should get going. Are you ready, Miss Honey?"

Miss Honey glanced up at her owner and then directed her liquid brown eyes at Romeo, who was quite obviously still captivated by her big-bellied, furry ways. This was not lost on Miss Honey and she pulled her lips back in what looked very much like a doggy grin.

Romeo yapped.

So Miss Honey gave him a single giant lick across his wet nose. Romeo's knees bowed.

Coral and Nicks grinned.

Ben grinned. "Happy treasure hunting!" he called out as he started jogging along the beach, clapping his hands for Miss Honey to follow. And like a good dog, she did exactly as she was told. Romeo watched her leave and whimpered.

While Ben and Miss Honey's shapes grew smaller and disappeared in one direction, a new shape appeared from the other. It grew bigger and bigger until it was finally Maggie Waterman, walking along the beach with her shoes dangling from the tip of one finger. She seemed relaxed and in no particular hurry.

"Mum!" cried Nicks.

"What are you doing here?!" crowed Coral at the top of her voice. Maggie Waterman looked alarmed. "I mean, er, shouldn't you be working at the Holiday Club with Mr Sparks?" she added in a calmer, gentler tone.

Nicks's mum pressed her collar down nervously, like she really didn't know what to make of her daughter and best friend any more. Their behaviour of late had seemed rather erratic to her. She watched them closely with a look that said, *I hope you two are not up to anything!*

"Yes, Mum – why aren't you with Mr Sparks?" echoed Nicks in frustration.

"I spent a few hours at the Holiday Club this morning," replied Nicks's mum defensively. "I said I would help and I'm very happy to do so. But I've also got a few things to do at the post office. It doesn't run itself, you know."

Coral wondered why Maggie Waterman was at the beach if this were true, but she knew it would be cheeky to ask so she made shapes in the sand with her toe instead.

"So when are you going back to Mr Sparks then?" asked Nicks.

"I'll be going back to *the Holiday Club* shortly," replied her mum with narrowed eyes.

"Oh, right. Oh good. Yes, that is good," mumbled Nicks.

"I came to ask you girls if you'd like something nice for your lunch and Meredith told me where to find you. But come to think of it, you can just head home for your usual cheese and Marmite sandwich." Maggie Waterman did not look pleased at all. Perhaps she'd had enough of being dressed up and pushed about.

Both girls' shoulders slumped. The cheese and Marmite sandwiches had nothing to do with their disappointment. After all, they were bound by their passion for Marmite. But they were finding it just about impossible to stir up any obvious interest between Mr Sparks and Maggie Waterman. They did not seem particularly interested in each other at all!

Coral stared dismally at the silver bucket of beach finds. The mermaid's purse gave her some very small comfort. It was definitely a good beach find; at least they'd got that right.

But Nicks was focused entirely on her mum. She stared at her and coughed to clear her throat. And then she took a very deep breath.

"Mum, are you going to take that job? Are we going to move far away from Sunday Harbour?"

Coral's head snapped up. She instantly forgot all about the mermaid's purse and stared at her friend, who looked like she might just cry.

Maggie Waterman was also looking at Nicks closely. She sighed deeply. "It's a great opportunity for me, Nicky-Nicks. Working in a post office was never my dream. But I have to consider you in this too. I could never forget that. So...well, honestly? I just don't know yet."

Playing for keeps

Romeo lay quietly with his soft pink belly pressed up against the deck of Coral Hut. His two front paws were curled over the edge of the decking and his dull, warm nose pointed at the horizon. He was awake, but might as well have been asleep. The sparkle had gone from his eyes and he was lifeless and miserable. He clearly had a bad dose of lovesickness. Coral patted his head compassionately. She felt sure they would see Miss Honey again – but of course she could offer no guarantees.

Just then Meredith emerged on to the deck of the beach hut next door. She was immediately followed by Malcolm, who was chuckling loudly.

"Oh, Merry, you are funny!" he said.

"No, Malcy, you're the funny one – my sides ache."

Merry? Malcy? Coral leaned forward to get a better view. She couldn't help herself.

"Well then, you're definitely the smartest person I know," countered Malcy with a cheeky grin.

Merry giggled. "No way – you are!"

Malcy grinned sideways and jiggled his eyebrows. "Well then, you are, without a doubt, the prettiest marine scientist around!"

Merry didn't seem interested in contesting this point. She smiled happily and touched Malcy's forearm lightly. Coral noticed that she was batting her eyelashes far more than usual.

She turned away from the gushing couple. *Great – there was love all around… but just not where it needed it to be!*

Nicks seemed oblivious to their newly touchy-feely neighbours. Like Romeo, she was also staring unfocused at the horizon. Coral knew that her friend was still thinking about the conversation she'd had with her mum. Coral knew this because Maggie Waterman's words were still ringing loudly in her ears too. She also knew Nicks well enough to know that her friend really needed some quiet time. Words were not always enough to make someone feel better. So Coral sat in her own puddle of silence and stared at nothing in particular. It wasn't much fun, but it did provide her with some of her own thinking time. And it wasn't long after this that her train of thought pulled in. *What they needed now was ACTION, not words!* Coral stood up. She dusted herself off. And then she looked around and grinned. Choo choo.

"Right, Nicky-Nicks, we're off to the Holiday Club then!"

Nicks barely budged. "Why?" she mumbled.

"Because we are not giving up yet, that's why. If Mr Sparks and your mum still haven't seen the potential in each other, then we'll have to point it out to them and make it very clear. C'mon, Cupid Company – let's matchmake!"

But nobody budged.

So Coral puffed out her chest and hollered as loud as a drill sergeant. "I saaaiiidd – let's matchmake!"

Coral led the way while Nicks and Romeo followed with their heels dragging. But Coral was not put off; she knew that all her friend and pup needed was to relax a little. So she took it upon herself to hum a tune while they walked all the way there.

The Summer Holiday Club met in the scout hall, and it was a noisy, busy place. There were small, scuffed brown tables pushed together to form one large, long table. Faded plastic chairs lined the walls and the chipped-tile floor was littered with slivers of colourful paper and drips of bright paint.

Most of the kids were armed with glue sticks or paintbrushes and were very busy being creative. Others were less interested in the arty side of things and more concerned with play fighting, telling jokes, swapping cards or fiddling with their mobile phones. Mr Sparks was at one end of the room and separating a boy from his football. Maggie Waterman was at the other end and hanging a shiny wet poster from a peg on string that was strung like a washing line across one corner of the hall. It looked like the sea star posters were coming along nicely.

Coral stared at the scene before her and thought carefully. They needed a plan. Since their encounter with Maggie Waterman that morning, Coral guessed that Maggie knew they were up to something. She was already dangerously suspicious and they could not risk creating even more suspicion in her mind.

"Nicks, you head over and help your mum with the posters."

Nicks stared at Coral dully. "That's your matchmaking plan?"

"We have to approach this carefully," replied Coral with narrowed eyes (which was a look she had learned from James Bond).

"So what should I say to her about Mr Sparks then?"

"You shouldn't say anything at all. Leave that to me – and Mr Sparks. Simply tell your mum we're here to help, and make general sea star chitchat."

Nicks considered this for a moment and then nodded. She ambled over to her mum, dodging an airborne paper plane along the way.

With that part of the plan in place, Coral finally turned to face Mr Sparks head on. She stood with her legs wide apart, her shoulders back and her spine stretched straight. Her hands rested quietly near her hips, open and ready. She flexed her fingers and cracked her knuckles. She was all set to fight for love (and she really did love her best friend Nicks very much).

"Come on, Romeo," she growled passionately. "Er, Romeo?"

The floor near her feet was empty. So she searched a little further until she found her pup. He was beneath a desk with his chin resting on his paws – staring ahead bleakly. But Coral couldn't think about his lovesickness now. She marched over to Mr Sparks and tapped him on the shoulder with her finger.

"Wha— oh, hello, Coral," he stammered. "What brings you here today?"

Coral sniffed and set her jaw. "We're here

to help... you know... with the sea star *and stuff.*"

"Oh good – that is useful. Superglue these sequins to this cardboard, won't you."

Coral set to work. "So how are things going with Maggie Waterman?" she enquired while she glued.

"Mrs Waterman is very efficient and helpful, thank you, Coral," replied Mr Sparks tersely.

And that's when it occurred to her. It all suddenly made sense. "Mrs Waterman is not really a Mrs – you do know that, don't you, Mr Sparks? You see, she wanted to keep the same name as Nicks because they're family... but she's definitely divorced... for, like, ages... so she's seriously completely over it... and er, him... her ex... that's Nicks's dad."

"Just keep on gluing, Coral," replied Mr Sparks.

"Yup, she really is a good mum like that," continued Coral. "Mrs Waterman is actually one of the most thoughtful, kindest, funniest, most intelligent people I've ever met. She's like a second mum to me."

"How very brave of her," mumbled Mr Sparks.

Not that Coral noticed. "And look how pretty she is, isn't she? It's unbelievable that she's still single – as in, no partner... uh, available. I mean, can you believe it?" Coral scratched her head theatrically, quite forgetting that her fingers were covered in superglue and sequins. She had to sacrifice hair to remove her fingers and it took all her inner strength not to cry out in pain. It also made attaching further sequins quite difficult. She wasn't used to working with hairy fingertips.

Mr Sparks seemed to be ignoring Coral, but that was OK because the pain had made Coral forget entirely where they were in this conversation anyway. "So, Mr Sparks," she groaned instead, "do you have any hobbies? I mean, like, what makes you happy?"

"I'm quite fond of peace and quiet," he replied quickly.

Coral stared at him blankly. *Peace and quiet was hardly a hobby.* And besides, he was a headteacher. He must have been joking about the peace and quiet thing. So she forced a loud laugh. He stared at her strangely.

"So what do you think about genes history then?" she asked, changing the subject.

"Pardon?"

"You know – family trees and stuff. It's when you trace your ancestors."

"You mean genealogy."

"Yep, Maggie Waterman is really into it. Hey, you're probably part Spanish – considering that you're into that cold Spanish soup."

"Gazpacho."

"Bless you."

"And I'm not."

"Not what?"

"Part Spanish."

"Well then you should definitely get Maggie Waterman to research your family tree. She could tell you what you are if you're not part Spanish."

Mr Sparks sighed loudly. "Coral, I am well aware of what I am, although I'm sure Mrs Waterman is a very talented lady."

"You mean Maggie," Coral corrected him. "And I'll be sure to tell her you said that." *Finally, progress.* Coral made a mental note to pass the compliment on. And then she remembered Merry and Malcy; a nickname was quite obviously a sign of affection. "Actually, you should call her Mags. She far prefers it."

Mr Sparks dropped his head and held it like it hurt. Coral did not want to lose him to a sudden headache; it was time to take it to the next level.

"You know, I think she might be lonely," she quickly added in a serious tone (it was a last resort she had hoped to avoid).

Mr Sparks's head snapped up. "Maggie – lonely?"

"You mean Mags." Coral then nodded sadly, as if to say, *I'm afraid so.*

Mr Sparks turned and chewed his lip thoughtfully for a few moments. He gazed across the hall, over the heads of the Holiday Club children, in the direction of Nicks and her mum. It just so happened that at that precise moment Mags Waterman was taking a break from the madness and staring out through the window at the view of the ocean. Anybody standing really close by would have noticed that the corners of her mouth were turned up. She was a little weary from all the hard work, but far from unhappy. However, from a distance there was a chance she might have looked detached and solemn.

"Loneliness can be a terrible thing," murmured Mr Sparks with cloudy eyes. "Perhaps I should invite Mags to join our Wii Get Fit Club?"

Coral remembered the cupboard beneath the stairs in Nicks's kitchen – the one filled with Mags' old tennis racket, flat-tyre bicycle and rusty abdominal exerciser.

"Erm, what other clubs do you belong to, Mr Sparks?"

Mr Sparks looked confused for a moment. "Other clubs? Well, the Draughts' Society meets every second Wednesday and—"

Coral grinned. *It took two people to play draughts!* "I think Mags would LOVE to accompany you on a draughts' evening!" She grinned some more. It was as good as a date. She really was a top matchmaker.

always and forever

Once the sea star posters were painted and dry, Coral and Nicks then helped the Holiday Club to put them up all around Sunday Harbour, in time for the Sea Life Aquarium Open Day. It was a sunny, fun-filled afternoon, although Mr Sparks didn't look quite so relaxed. He seemed to be focused on orbiting around Coral, as if he daren't get too close.

The following few days were also dedicated

to the Aquarium Open Day. Coral's mum in particular raced around red-cheeked and slightly out of breath; there were still some last-minute jobs to be done and she was not one to say no. Coral and Nicks did as much as they could; if nothing else, it helped to keep their thoughts occupied. Romeo benefitted from the busyness too, and although he seemed to be always on the lookout for Miss Honey, all the activity did him good.

The whirlwind of Open Day activity finally died down on the afternoon before the big event. The trestle tables were at long last in place. Triangle flags attached to rope now hung suspended – with those outside gaily flapping and flicking in the sea breeze. There were helium foil balloons hanging on by a string and decorative giant cardboard cut-outs of colourful cartoon sea creatures. Ordinary white light bulbs had been replaced by orange, blue and yellow bulbs which gave everything a warm, beachy glow. And instead of pinning the tail on the donkey, young children would soon be entertained by pinning the claw on the crab.

Finally everyone left for home, except for Coral and Nicks. They had wandered down to their beach hut to enjoy the sights and sounds of the end of the day from the deck. Merry and Malcy arrived at the beach not long afterwards. They were giggling and talking in hushed voices and only seemed to notice the girls when Coral shouted out hello.

"Oh, hiya!" Meredith waved back. She did seem surprised, almost like she'd forgotten there were other people on Earth.

"Hey, girls – we have the metal detector. Would you like to have a go with it now?" called Malcolm. The man's face was one giant grin.

As a professional in the field of love, Coral instantly recognised that his smile had very little to do with lending them the metal

200

detector. And despite all the trouble love was giving them at the moment, it was still one of her very favourite things in the world, so she grinned back. And then she turned to face her friend with raised eyebrows.

Nicks shrugged. "Mmm, we already have the mermaid's purse. I think that's a pretty good beach find, don't you?"

Coral seemed to consider this for a moment. *Was it good enough to win the ingenious Scientific Weather Forecaster?* "It is a good find," she agreed. "But I still want to be a metal detective. Come on, let's give it another go."

Nicks shrugged for a second time and climbed to her feet. Romeo instantly jumped up on his four paws too. The last time they'd gone treasure hunting he'd met Miss Honey and it seemed like there was no way he was going to miss this expedition! He yapped excitedly.

Malcy disappeared inside their red beach hut and soon reappeared carrying the flying saucer at the end of a pole. "Good luck, girls," he said as he handed it over to Coral (who was making breathless 'me me' sounds while she hopped about with her arms extended).

Coral grabbed a firm hold of the metal handle and tested the weight of the detector with her arms. It felt good. She was most definitely a metal detective. She had just turned in the direction of the shoreline when Merry called out.

"Hey, girls, the most valuable treasure is often the sort of thing people have dropped or lost... so search the areas of the beach where people tend to hang about."

"You mean like around the deckchairs?" suggested Nicks loudly.

Merry nodded. "And around the rocks, for example."

The girls nodded and set off with Romeo trailing closely. They didn't have very much time; the sun was already beginning to slide down the sky. Dusk was not far away.

The first beep-beep of the metal detector led them straight to a lead fishing weight that was buried in shallow sand. It was unexceptional, but the girls picked it up anyway; after all, they had decided to decorate the hut's railing with their beach finds. The second beep-beep came soon after. This time they found a coin. It was new and didn't have great value, but they kept this too. They wandered around for a while before they heard a third beep-beep. The girls immediately wondered if this find would be worth the wait. It was certainly buried deeper. Nicks scratched around in the sand for a few moments and then held her arm up in the air victoriously.

"It's a watch!" she cried out.

It definitely was a watch. Coral was just as excited and couldn't wait to take a look (she was imagining a fashionable, expensive bling-bling sort of watch). They brushed the damp sand from the watch glass, which was broken. The hour hand was missing and the watch face was plastic. It was not even imitation bling-bling or remotely fashionable. It was just a cheap, broken watch.

"I think this was thrown away, not lost," mumbled a fed-up Coral. "Litterbugs."

The afternoon had grown late and it was getting chilly. "Let's head back," suggested the more sensible of the two friends.

Coral shivered and nodded her agreement. Being a metal detective was not as much fun covered in goosebumps. So they hiked through the sand back up to the beach huts. They still had to return the metal detector, so Coral and Nicks stood at the bottom of the steps to their neighbours hut while Coral called out loudly.

"Malcy... er, Malcolm?"

She waited, but only heard silence.

"Meredith?"

She waited a little longer. There was still no answer. So she climbed the red steps leading up to the deck of their hut and knocked on the door. And then she waited some more. But still nothing and nobody stirred. Coral glanced around the deck and decided against simply leaving the machine. What if it disappeared? So she trudged back down the steps with the detector in tow.

Then she heard Merry's flirty giggle. It was coming from the promenade, behind the huts.

"Meredith!" Coral called out once more. Maybe they were just leaving and on their way home?

"Come on, Nicks." Coral decided to catch them by taking the quickest route – she would nip underneath Coral Hut, which stood tall on four stilts, and then shimmy up the small bank to the promenade.

She and Nicks moved their legs double-time. And then, all of a sudden, just as they reached the very centre of the shadowy space directly beneath Coral Hut, the metal detector gave a loud beep-beep sound. Coral froze instantly (she hadn't even realised that she'd left the machine switched on!). She stood for a moment, unmoving, while the machine continued with its beep-beeping. Coral glanced at Nicks. The sand was dark and cool beneath the beach hut. It was a place she had never visited before. And then they dropped to their knees and started digging.

They had to dig through at least a foot of sand before they came to a metal box. It was black and chipped with red-rust blotches around the hinges. Coral's thoughts moved as quickly as her fingers. *Had they finally found real treasure?* The damp sand had eaten into the metal, making it rough and stiff. Coral fumbled with the catch on the box, until finally it came apart in her hand. She lifted the lid, which moved surprisingly easily, to find that the box was filled with a wodge of oil cloth.

Coral was moving too quickly to be disappointed just yet. Carefully, she removed the oil cloth and opened it up, fold by fold, to reveal two matching silver heart-shaped pendants on chains. She looked across at Nicks. The silver was tarnished and a dull, dark colour, but there was no mistaking this treasure. The old black and white photograph of Great-Aunt Coral standing beside her best friend Betty on the deck of Coral Hut filled her head entirely – almost as if she was right there beside them. Her eyes pricked with tears. She sucked in her breath and held it. *They had found Betty and Great-Aunt Coral's friendship necklaces!* The girls must have buried them beneath Coral Hut before Betty moved away. Perhaps this was the only way they could remain together forever, at their favourite place in Sunday Harbour.

checkmate

Coral passed the dulled silver-grey pendants over to Nicks and her friend rubbed her thumb across the letters engraved into the metal. One pendant was etched with a B, the other with a letter C. Nicks's thumb lingered longest on the pendant inscribed with a C. She imagined that her Great-Aunt Betty would have worn this pendant to remind her of her very best friend. It was how friendship necklaces worked. It was a way of keeping her best friend close to her heart. And although Nicks had never met her great-aunt, for a short moment she felt like they were close – that she was almost touching her.

Finally Nicks glanced up and found Coral's eyes. They had matching trickles of tears running down their cheeks.

And then Coral grinned wider than she'd ever grinned before. Her smile was like a light that illuminated her face. "So this has to be, like, the best beach find in the world!" she cried out, although she wasn't for one moment even thinking about winning the ingenious Scientific Weather Forecaster. They were holding a piece of their history, and getting this close to Betty and Coral made their great-aunts seem real. There could be no other treasure quite like this one.

"So what do we do now?" wondered Nicks.

Coral stared down at the pendants once more. Truth be told, she still felt slightly overwhelmed by their find. She knew the strength and meaning of true friendship. Just like their great-aunts, Coral and Nicks were really close. But their great-aunts buried these pendants because they were about to be separated forever. And as silly as it might have seemed, a small voice inside Coral's head feared that the pendants might bring them the same tragic luck. The same voice said that they should not separate the pendants.

"Maybe we should keep them here – in Coral Hut, for tonight, at least. After all, this was Coral and Betty's very favourite place in the world too."

Nicks seemed to consider this for a quiet moment. And then she nodded. "I agree," she said softly.

Coral smiled gently at her friend. "But we won't leave the pendants in this rusted box, wrapped up in that old cloth. Just wait a moment." She disappeared inside the beach hut and returned carrying Great-Aunt Coral's old keepsakes box and a few pieces of soft pink tissue paper. Then she gently wrapped the pendants up and placed them inside the box. "There, that's much better," she said.

Suddenly there was a knock on the open beach hut door. It was lovey-dovey Malcolm and Meredith.

"There you girls are!" cried Malcolm. "We've been searching the beach for you two."

Of course Coral and Nicks had been searching for them as well, but in all the recent excitement they'd pretty much forgotten this fact.

"Is everything all right?" asked Nicks.

"Oh, definitely," replied Meredith. "It's just that your mum popped by the beach hut while you were out metal detecting, Nicks. She was looking for you, but seemed to be in a bit of a hurry. So we said we'd pass a message on."

Coral and Nicks remained silent and expectant.

Meredith stared back at them, silent and smiling.

After a few more moments of silence, Malcolm chuckled and nudged Meredith gently with his elbow. "Silly you – give them the message."

"Oh, silly me!" agreed Meredith. "Old Mrs Forgetful!"

Malcolm hooked his arm through old Mrs Forgetful's arm. "You mean *wonderful* Mrs Forgetful."

Meredith giggled and blushed a rose colour. "Oh Malcy, you say the sweetest things."

"No, you do."

"No – you!"

Coral and Nicks rolled their eyes at the heavens. Love rocked (and they did take some credit for this particular love affair), *but could they have their message, please!*

Malcy must have noticed their impatience because he quickly filled in the blanks. "Nicks, your mum said to tell you that she is off to play darts tonight but not to worry because she's already arranged for you to have dinner at Coral's house."

The girls turned to each other. *Darts?*

"Oh, Malcy – now you're old Mr Forgetful. It was draughts, not darts!"

Suddenly old Mr and Mrs Forgetful started hooting with laughter – like this was the funniest thing ever. It definitely wasn't the funniest thing ever, but Coral whooped along with them anyway. Nicks and Romeo were the only two non-whoopers there that day. After all, Nicks still had no idea why her mother should be off playing draughts all of a sudden. And Romeo was still lovesick and miserable.

"Thank you very much for the message!" Coral finally managed through whoop-shaped lips.

"Alrighty then, see you tomorrow at the Open Day," replied Meredith as they turned to leave.

Coral spied the metal detector still leaning against the deck railings and called out to

Malcolm, who picked it up as he went past. And then Coral turned to her best friend. "Come on," she said, "let's head home. I'll tell you all about your mum and the draughts game along the way."

Nicks nodded patiently and leaned over to pat Romeo's sad little head. "You know, I don't think that he can go on in this way," she murmured. "We're going to have to find Miss Honey."

Coral locked the beach hut doors and stared down at her pup, who was moping along with a bent tail and droopy ears. "You're quite right, Nicky-Nicks. And I think that we should make it a Cupid Company priority." He really did look quite miserable.

The girls set off for home. "We should have asked Ben where he worked," considered Nicks while she walked. "That would have been useful."

"I wonder if we should get Ben to fill out a Cupid Company questionnaire on behalf of

Miss Honey first," replied Coral. "After all, love at first sight does not always work out in the long term." And then she laughed (although as an expert in the field of love she was only half-joking about the love at first sight thing... it really was no guarantee).

"Maybe we should arrange a proper first date for the pups," giggled Nicks in reply.

Coral smiled and draped her arm across the shoulders of her very best friend. "Speaking of first dates," she began, "that game of draughts..."

Coral explained while the girls strolled into the sunset. And then – finally – Nicks whooped and jump-clicked her heels together. Now it really looked as if the Cupid Company only had Romeo to worry about.

friends indeed

"Isn't it just the most perfect weather for an open day," cooed Maggie Waterman as she unpacked the hand-painted banner from the boot of her car. It was still early morning, but already the promenade and its surrounds hummed with activity. Everyone looked forward to this special day in the calendar; there wasn't anyone in Sunday Harbour who didn't love the ocean and the aquarium.

Nicks, however, didn't look particularly pleased – but the weather and ocean had very little to do with her unhappiness. In fact, she'd barely even noticed the clear and calm blue skies or the softly glowing sun. Not even the happily screeching seagulls seemed to cheer her up.

"You're not still miserable about my draughts evening, are you?" Nicks's mum asked her daughter.

Nicks shrugged. She tried not to scowl, but she couldn't help it. Yesterday she'd been so excited, today much less so. It was like her mum had stomped all over her hope until there was nothing left of it.

"So what if I didn't particularly enjoy the evening? Draughts is obviously just not my sort of game."

"Well, I think it was very kind of Mr Sparks to invite you along," grumbled Nicks. "He obviously likes you very much."

Maggie Waterman thought about this for a

moment. "Mmm. He is nice enough. But he did talk a lot about being lonely. Poor man. And he does seem to enjoy playing board games." She scrunched her nose up at this, like she didn't much enjoy board games herself.

Nicks frowned. It seemed as though Coral's plan had backfired (it would not be the first time either!). But Nicks would not give up while there was still the faintest smidgen of a glimmer of hope. "Well, Mum, if Mr Sparks is lonely, then isn't that all the more reason for you to give the draughts one more go?"

"Of course I'd like to stay friendly with Mr Sparks," replied Maggie Waterman thoughtfully. "But we have very little in common."

If Nicks's face was scowling before, now it was positively thunderous. She shut the car door with a firm thud and stamped in the direction of the aquarium. "You haven't even given Mr Sparks a chance..." she muttered as she stamped. But Maggie Waterman was too busy admiring her hand-painted SIGN UP FOR THE SEA STAR banner to notice. She seemed to be very proud of her efforts.

Coral had been looking out for Nicks and she met her friend wearing a matching frown.

"So no change with your mum then, I suppose?" she asked hopefully.

Nicks shook her head. "Nope. She still doesn't seem interested in draughts or Mr Sparks at all. In fact, I think she feels sorry for him more than anything."

"Sorry for him?" murmured Coral. "That doesn't sound too good—"

But Nicks just raised her hand in the air. There was no point in discussing the matter any further. The Cupid Company had failed, it was that simple. Time was running out and now there was no reason for her mum to consider staying in Sunday Harbour.

Coral's mum sailed past in a flurry of To Do lists. She had a pen stuck behind each ear and green paper streamers tangled around her left ankle. There was a torn, folded poster climbing out of the back pocket of her jeans and a smudge of blue paint across her right cheek. She did look very busy indeed.

"I really could do with some help," she called out to the girls as she went.

They shrugged. Why not? Now that the Cupid Company had officially crashed and burned in their task, what else did they have to occupy their time with?

"Just coming..." they mumbled miserably.

"Where's Romeo then?" asked Nicks while they scrambled to catch up with Coral's flying mum.

"He's off moping," replied Coral. "We really do need to find Miss Honey... and soon."

Finally they caught up with Coral's mum at the aquarium cafe, where there was a special Open Day menu offering ocean-themed dishes like clam chowder, scallop salad, barbecue shrimp and crab cakes with seafood sauce. Devoted land lovers, however, could still enjoy other dishes like kebabs, fajitas, chickpea burgers, fresh fruit and muffins while Mr Gelatti prepared to sell ice cream from one of the big silver freezers. That was, until the freezer suddenly stopped humming. Then Mr Gelatti looked as hot and bothered as the ice cream that was quickly melting.

"There's a problem with the motor," groaned Coral's mum. "I need to stay here and wait for help. Could you girls please take this over to Mrs Nesbitt? She's manning the Best Beach Finds table, just beyond the Touch Tank." She waved a piece of paper in the general direction.

Coral reached for the piece of paper, but stayed silent. *The Best Beach Finds competition! With all that had been going on she really hadn't given it much thought lately.*

"Come on, maybe we can ask around for Miss Honey along the way," said Nicks, who was still looking glum but had resolved to make the most of what little time she had left in Sunday Harbour – and that went for her work at the Cupid Company too.

Coral had also resolved to give her all to today's event and finding Miss Honey, but her reasons were quite different. Thinking about something else was the only way she could stop thinking about Nicks leaving. So they ambled over to Mrs Nesbitt at the Best Beach Finds table and handed her the piece of paper. And then they took a long look at the table of beach finds.

There was a wooden fish box, cuttlebones of a cuttlefish, a violet shell of a sea snail, a polystyrene float covered in barnacles and a broken piece of a turtle's shell. There was even a dried-up seahorse that had probably washed ashore. Coral stared at the lifeless creature. *Seahorse? It didn't even look like a horse.* The starfish wasn't the only priority then.

The rest of the table was filled with a less than impressive collection of seashells, smoothed pebbles, a very large rusted bolt and one dented thermos flask with its lid missing. And then Coral saw it – the ingenious Scientific Weather Forecaster. It stood grandly, upright and in its box, which had a clear plastic front so that passers-by could admire the contraption in all its glory. It was silver and shiny and covered in small dials with buttons and gauges. It was even more impressive than she could ever have imagined.

But for all of the Forecaster's glory, Coral remained silent. Nicks didn't speak a word either. As very best friends, they really didn't need to.

Our mermaid's purse might be – could be – the best beach find here today, pondered Nicks.

There can be no better beach find than two silver friendship pendants, reflected Coral.

But those pendants are special; perhaps too special for a Best Beach Finds competition?

Yes, definitely far too special to be left on a table with a dried-up old seahorse and a thermos flask that doesn't even have a lid.

"So I'll fetch the mermaid's purse then, shall I?" said Nicks out loud.

Coral nodded her agreement and eyed up the Forecaster one last time. No matter how much she wanted to make its shiny forecasting abilities her own, sometimes there were just more important things than winning.

smiles to last forever

There was less than an hour to go before the official opening of the Aquarium Open Day, although the time seemed to fly by in a matter of minutes. But a SIGN UP FOR THE SEASTAR banner was suspended across a wall, stalls were hurriedly readied and aquarium staff and volunteers finally stood alert at their posts. Everyone seemed very pleased with the progress that had been made – everyone except for two girls. Coral and Nicks had mingled thoroughly and kept a careful lookout for Ben and Miss Honey, but with no luck. And of course Mr Sparks (who was helping out at the raffle booth) and Maggie Waterman (who was preparing to collect sea star petition signatures) still had not exchanged anything more than a friendly but very casual hello. Coral and Nicks knew this because they'd been watching them very carefully too.

The rest of the Sunday Harbour folk were all lined up outside and eager to come inside the aquarium. It was the mayor who finally opened the doors. She was met by enthusiastic smiles, some polite jostling and a lot of excited chatter. The line of visitors rapidly dispersed as people made for the reef pool, underwater tunnel or the Touch Tank. The aquarium cafe remained empty though; there was still way too much to see for anyone to think about food just yet. Trembling fingers pointed at the scuba divers swimming alongside the sharks in the huge half-moon tank. Children giggled at the sea lions, who were as funny as they were clever. The manta rays put on a show to music and moved their little mouths as if singing. Fish were fed to the sounds of clapping and cheering. And in the Touch Tank barnacles were rubbed, anemones got a tickle and hermit crabs swapped shells.

Coral and Nicks divided their time between enjoying the sights and sounds of the bustling aquarium, and helping out where and when they were needed. They collected a few petition signatures, helped to sort the children's goody bags and carried buckets of cut-up fish ready for feeding time. Romeo tried to help. He even tried to enjoy himself. But after a while he gave up trying and simply followed the girls with his head bent low. Coral was just about to rub his ears soothingly when Mrs Nesbitt suddenly called out to them. She'd been given a message from Coral's mum, who had just seen Meredith at the dolphin pool: the girls were needed urgently! After all, somebody had to hold the hoops for the dolphins to jump through. This was exciting news and the girls raced all the way over to the pool. And there, quite unexpectedly, stood Ben – Miss Honey's owner. The girls came to a screeching halt and stared in surprise. Of course, Miss Honey was right beside Ben, wearing a rather spectacular glittery studded collar and lead. She appeared to have been washed and brushed and looked more furry and beautiful than ever.

Romeo sniffed the air. He spied Miss Honey. His spine snapped straight. He flipped his head high and pointed his nose to the sky. And then he let out an almighty howl. He was quite obviously one happy and very excited pup. He strained with all his might to get closer to Miss Honey. Coral tightened her grip on his lead, although of course she was not one to get in the way of true love. Laughing out loud, she stumbled as she managed to keep a hold on the determined pup. Miss Honey, meanwhile, played it cooler (although her tail gave her away – it wagged so fast it was a blur).

The two pups met and touched noses. And then Romeo covered Miss Honey's snout in little licks of his pink tongue. She closed her eyes and seemed to enjoy every moment. It really was true love. The girls chuckled.

"Romeo has missed Miss Honey!" cried Coral happily.

Ben laughed too. "And Miss Honey has been off her food these past few days. I thought she might be coming down with something, but now I see that she's been pining for your pup all along!"

Coral noticed the AQUARIUM MANAGER

229

badge pinned to Ben's shirt. So this was how he knew all about the mermaid's purse! Just then Meredith pointed at the girls and announced that the dolphins were ready to jump through hoops.

But who would look after Romeo? The girls glanced left and right. And then Maggie Waterman came strolling past, carrying her clipboard of sea star petition forms. "Mum, could you hang on to Romeo for a little while, please!" cried Nicks.

Maggie Waterman looked momentarily confused and then shrugged and accepted the pup's lead. She watched the two girls race off in the direction of the dolphin pool and then slowly turned to face the man standing beside her. He was very tall and her eyes travelled upwards until they finally settled on his lovely face. And then she smiled. And then she looked embarrassed. She looked away, back down to Romeo, and gave his lead a gentle tug like they really should be going.

But Romeo would not budge. It didn't look like Miss Honey was going anywhere fast either.

Ben laughed. "I think we're stuck with each other for a while!" he said. If his smile was anything to go by, he didn't seem to mind very much either.

Maggie Waterman stood silent and unmoving. If she'd barely heard him then it was because she was far too busy admiring his lovely white smile.

"I'm Ben, by the way." He held his hand out.

Maggie stared at his hand and gave a silly sort of grin. "And I'm Maggie," she finally replied.

Nicks collected the hoops while Coral stared breathlessly across the dolphin pool at the pups and the two people holding their leads. Ben chatted away while Maggie giggled every so often. And then Maggie said something to make Ben laugh. Coral watched them for a short while longer. She was a seasoned matchmaker; she knew that different smiles meant different things. And these happy smiles looked very promising indeed...

peas in a pod

The dolphins jumped through the hoops without missing a single one. Coral liked to think that this was because of the way she and Nicks held the hoops out like expert hoop holders. Nicks was laughing at the same time. They were covered in salt-water spray, and she found watching the dolphins sail past at nose height quite exhilarating.

When they were done with hoop holding,

the girls stuck close to Malcolm and Meredith and offered their help at every (and any) opportunity. Of course they were having a blast, but there was no way they were going to separate Ben and Maggie (or Miss Honey and Romeo) just yet! So it was important they kept busy and well away from the well-matched pairs. And it was only much later, right towards the end of the day, that they finally claimed Romeo back from Nicks's mum. Not that she appeared to mind puppysitting one bit. Her cheeks were rosy and her eyes shone. Ben also appeared a little shinier and perkier than before. The girls sent each other secret grins. *Were they on to a winner?* And then, just when it seemed like this might be the best day ever, Mr Sparks appeared from out of nowhere. He did not look shiny or perky and seemed quite stiff and very stern by comparison.

He stared at Ben for a brief moment and then nodded politely before turning his full attention to Nicks's mum. He cleared his throat. "Maggie, do you think I could have a word with you in private, please?"

Maggie stared at Mr Sparks with wide eyes. Ben watched Maggie. Coral and Nicks blinked nervously and gawped at Maggie, Mr Sparks and Ben in turn. Finally Maggie nodded her reply and fell in line with Mr Sparks, who ushered Maggie past the half-moon tank, in the direction of the cafe. The girls turned to each other.

Mr Sparks is going to ruin everything!

And we were so close!

Suddenly a voice rumbled through a set of loudspeakers. "Ladies and gentleman, could you please all make your way over to the presentation area where we will declare the winner of the Best Beach Finds competition." The voice was Malcolm's.

The public announcement seemed to startle Ben, who suddenly stood ramrod straight. "Ah no!" he cried out. "I'm the new – and rather late – aquarium manager," he added apologetically. "I need you girls to look after Miss Honey for me, please. I won't be long."

Nicks nodded glumly. Of course they'd look after Miss Honey. That was no trouble at all. But first her mum had been dragged away; now Ben was doing a disappearing act. And it had all been going so well.

"Come on, Nicks," said Coral who, despite everything, had not forgotten entirely about the ingenious Scientific Weather Forecaster.

A crowd had gathered in the presentation area and the girls managed to squeeze into an empty space somewhere close to the front. The pups did not seem to mind where they went, as long as they went there together. Ben arrived at the same time and clambered on to the small, raised stage. He then aimed his winning smile at the audience, coughed twice, and began to talk about the wonderful day they had all shared and what it meant to the aquarium and the sea star (although he only included the sea star after a fierce-look prompt by Malcolm, who was hopping about in the background and seemed strangely agitated).

Coral and Nicks tried to concentrate, but they looked around frantically. *Where were Mr Sparks and Maggie Waterman?*

Now Ben was talking about marine conservation and how important it was to a seaside town like Sunday Harbour. He felt sure that everyone would do their bit. And then, finally, he turned his attention to the table of beach finds.

"Our runner's-up prize," he announced, "is the mermaid's purse, submitted by Coral, Nicks and Romeo." He scanned the crowd, looking for the girls.

Coral's eyes were closed and her fingers crossed. She opened one eye and tilted her head. Had she heard correctly? She hadn't been expecting the runner's-up prize.

But Ben seemed to think that the

runner's-up prize was just brilliant. He grinned and waved an envelope in the air. "You girls have won free entry to the aquarium for one whole year," he revealed proudly.

Nicks smiled and, sensing that Coral was not moving any time soon, quickly squeezed though the crowd to accept their free passes with a polite thank you. Ben waited patiently for her to return to her place before continuing. Malcolm, meanwhile, hopped around in the background and seemed to be nervously chewing his fingers.

"And the winner of the Best Beach Finds competition and the Scientific Weather Forecaster is…" Ben scanned the crowd for a particular face, "…Mr Selvaggio from Deli Antonia!"

The girls turned to each other. *Mr Selvaggio!*

"Well done for finding the giraffe seahorse, Mr Selvaggio," continued Ben with a pleased-as-punch expression. "I must say, this is a most exceptional and rather rare find."

Now Coral turned to Nicks. *The giraffe seahorse?* That old dried-up seahorse that had been sitting on the table? Suddenly, the sea star campaign seemed almost pointless by comparison.

But nobody else seemed to think that the giraffe seahorse was a strange sort of thing, and Mr Selvaggio seemed very happy to collect his ingenious Scientific Weather Forecaster. Coral stared unhappily at the prize, nestled in his grip. She'd been beaten by a seahorse that wasn't a horse and didn't even look like a giraffe.

Suddenly Malcolm – who was still loitering in the background and now running his hands through his hair anxiously – sidled up close to Ben and prised the microphone from the aquarium manager's grip. He then tapped the microphone and blew into it twice.

"Excuse me, everyone?"

The excited crowd quickly quietened down again.

Now that Malcolm had the crowd's attention he suddenly seemed even more nervous. He chuckled and gulped down a few deep breaths.

"Meredith, could you please join me up on stage," he began, and paused, waiting for his co-campaigner – who had been directing a mum with a small boy to the nearest toilets. She glanced up, surprised, and then negotiated the crowd to the stage. Smiling a nervous, lopsided sort of smile, she stared out across the room packed with expectant faces. There was a reason why she had not got involved in the prize-giving in the first place. She suffered with stage fright. She looked confused and lost too. So she raised a hand and waved sheepishly at the people of Sunday Harbour.

"Erm, Meredith," Malcolm finally continued. And then he took another deep breath and dropped to one knee. "Make me the happiest man in the world and marry me, please?"

Meredith froze, her waving hand still in the air.

The crowd gasped. And then fell silent.

Malcolm waited with oily white cheeks and eyes as big as two small planets.

"I... uh..." stammered Meredith in a breathy voice. "Oh, Malcy, of course I will!"

The people of Sunday Harbour instantly erupted with an almighty cheer and Coral and Nicks clapped louder than anyone. After all, thanks to their romantic picnic these two best friends and research partners had finally looked at each other with love in their eyes. And of course, there was no better cause for celebration than true love.

Malcolm and Meredith kissed and hugged and shared one more kiss before they were swallowed up by the tide of well-wishers. Malcolm received hearty whacks on the back and Meredith's cheeks turned pink from all the kisses she collected.

But still there was no sign of Mr Sparks or Maggie Waterman. And then finally they appeared – two lone shapes striding down the corridor from the direction of the cafe. Nicks spied them first and she elbowed Coral, who stared long and hard until finally she could see their faces clearly. Mr Sparks looked serene and satisfied. Maggie Waterman had a smile-shaped mouth and shiny eyes. *Had they finally decided to fall in love too?* It was all a bit of a mystery and the girls tunnelled through the crowd with an 'excuse me, please excuse me' as they went. They were breathless by the time their paths crossed with Mr Sparks and Maggie Waterman.

"Mum!" cried Nicks. And then she seemed at a loss. "Is uh, everything all right?"

Maggie Waterman laughed. "All right? I'd say so!" She turned and smiled at Mr Sparks.

"How all right is it exactly then?" wondered Coral, who thought she might burst a blood vessel from not knowing *what was going on!*

Mr Sparks smiled back at Maggie Waterman and then gave the top of her hand a gentle little pat. "I have just offered Maggie a teaching post at our school," he revealed. "I will be taking a sabbatical – I'm going to teach in India for a year. And I need someone to teach my history pupils."

Nicks stared at her mum, too terrified to even ask. So Coral did.

"And have you accepted?"

Maggie Waterman tilted her head and glanced up at the stage area just at the exact moment that Ben, who had been shaking Malcolm's hand in congratulations, glanced down in the direction of their small group. They smiled at each other.

Maggie coughed and quickly refocused her attention on the two very eager faces before her. "Yes, girls, I have definitely accepted," she finally replied.

Coral and Nicks whooped louder than ever before and squeezed each other tightly. They were both crying big fat tears but were too happy to even notice their sodden cheeks. Nicks then hugged her mum and Coral flung her arms around Mr Sparks without actually meaning to. They stood – cheek by cheek – for a few awkward, silent moments before Coral peeled herself from her headteacher. And then she turned to her best friend's mum, who had practically been like a mum to her.

"Congratulations, Mrs – erm, Maggie Waterman," she said in a grown-up voice. "I hope you will be very happy as our new history teacher."

Maggie Waterman grinned and put her arm around the shoulders of the girl who was almost like a daughter to her, and they started walking. So Coral seized the moment.

"While we're on the subject of history as a school subject," she began, "I should probably mention that I tend to get my King Henrys mixed up. I'm still not sure I understand what happened when Norman invaded either. Oh, and do you think we could bother a little less with dates? I've never been very good at remembering dates..."

SOUL MATES

There was only one way to end the best day ever, and that was at the best place ever – Nicks and Coral's beloved beach hut. The late-afternoon sun had painted the sky with gold streaks as it travelled to the other side of the world. But it was still light and warm and there were plenty of Sunday Harbour folk about. There was a group of teenagers playing touch rugby in the sand. An old couple sitting in matching deckchairs snoozed with their heads back, their faces covered by matching straw hats. Two barefoot joggers stopped suddenly, dropped to the sand and did sit-ups with their toes touching the water. And just below Coral Hut – in a small dip at the bottom of the hut's steps – lay Romeo and Miss Honey basking in the fading sun and their obvious love for each other. Romeo's furry head rested on Miss Honey's front paws while Miss Honey's chin balanced tenderly on his head. They were like a little love sandwich.

Coral smiled and turned to face her very best, very dearest friend in the whole, entire planet (and universe and beyond). She glowed just as much as the golden sky above. She was pleased; it looked like love really had won the day.

Coral's grin was not lost on Nicks. She grinned back happily and jerked a thumb at the two love-struck pups. "Aren't they the sweetest!" she crooned.

The best friends laughed. "He deserves every bit of happiness too," agreed Coral smugly. "After all, it's thanks to our Romeo that your mum and Ben met each other in the first place. If Romeo hadn't fallen in love with Miss Honey and been so determined to stick by her side... well, Maggie and Ben may have just walked right on past each other."

Nicks nodded. "Yup, he's definitely earned his place in the Cupid Company."

"Maybe he should be MD – you know, managing dog," chuckled Coral.

"He is *the love doggy*!" The girls giggled. "And what about Meredith and Malcolm?" added Nicks excitedly. "Thanks to the Cupid Company and our fabulously romantic picnic, we helped to create yet another match made in heaven."

"Yes, you can never underestimate a really good, romantic picnic," murmured Coral thoughtfully. "But I'd like to have a serious word with Malcolm and Meredith." She frowned slightly.

"Why, what about?"

"I think we've been cheated. What I mean is... our mermaid's purse lost out to a giraffe seahorse."

Nicks shrugged. She clearly did not understand.

"*A giraffe seahorse!*" repeated Coral indignantly. "As if the name seahorse isn't misleading enough... now we have a *giraffe* seahorse. It's all quite silly and just like the starfish, until this sea creature has a new, *proper* name, it really should not be entering into any competitions." And then she mumbled something about the ingenious Scientific Weather Forecaster, but her words were cut short by Nicks's cry.

"Hey, there's Mr Selvaggio! And it looks like he's got the Weather Forecaster with him."

"He's probably come to gloat," scowled Coral as she watched him trudging up the beach in the direction of their beach hut. The deli owner paused at the bottom step and waited patiently for the love-struck pups to let him pass. When it became clear that they had no intention of parting, not even a millimetre, he carefully stepped up and over them.

"Hello-a Coral. Hello-a Nicks," he said, except he got it the wrong way round. But neither of the girls corrected him. Coral (who was actually Nicks) smiled warmly while Nicks (who was actually Coral) glowered at the ingenious Scientific Weather Forecaster (or she glowered at the box it was in, anyway).

"I have-a no time for any community spirit questions today, I'm afraid, but I have-a come with a proposition for you girls," continued Mr Selvaggio with the outline of an anxious frown pressed to his forehead. "I wonder if you'd be interested in-a swapping your free aquarium passes with my Scientific Weather Forecaster?"

And then he fell silent. So were the girls.

They stared at him closely. *Was he being serious?*

Mr Selvaggio shrugged sheepishly. "I own a deli. What do-a I care what tomorrow's weather will bring?" That was his entire argument.

Coral turned to Nicks and shrugged too. *The man has a point.*

Nicks shrugged in reply. *My mum and Ben already seem to be rather good friends – and then of course there's Romeo and Miss Honey – we'll probably get free passes to the aquarium anyway!*

Coral nodded thoughtfully. Nicks chewed her bottom lip thoughtfully. And then they both turned to face Mr Selvaggio.

"DEAL!" they both said at once.

Nicks had already buried their free passes in the keepsakes box for safekeeping and she disappeared inside the hut to retrieve the box. Coral stood and stared at the Forecaster. And then she opened her arms like a mum whose baby was returning home. *Finally!*

251

Nicks reappeared and handed the aquarium passes over to their new owner. Mr Selvaggio grinned and tipped his hat. "It's been-a great doing business with you ladies. Bye bye now." And then he was gone.

Nicks went back rooting around in the keepsakes box. Coral, meanwhile, wrestled with the box containing the Forecaster. With a few more tugs and a small tear in the cardboard, the Forecaster was finally revealed in all its ingenious glory. It was silver and very shiny. Coral eyed it up carefully. It really did look quite complicated. Illuminated numbers flashed importantly. There were plenty of percentage figures, all of which meant nothing to her. And as for the bar graph – it featured one mysterious symbol after the next.

Coral picked up the Forecaster's instruction manual. It was as thick as a telephone directory and opened up on a detailed index of complicated weather icons.

"Swiss high-definition sensor..." she

murmured out loud as she read. Her brow furrowed with a deep frown. "Variable LCD contrast... or something... mmm."

She snapped the instruction manual shut and abandoned it on a nearby deckchair. "So how about today then... what a really great day, huh!" she said brightly to Nicks, who seemed to be focused on something else entirely. The keepsakes box was open on her lap and she held a very small, dark green hardcover book in her hands.

"*Forever Love*," she read out loud.

"What is that?" asked Coral as she moved closer.

Finally Nicks looked up. "It's a book of poetry called *Forever Love*. I found it in Great-Aunt Coral's old keepsakes box. I'd never noticed it before."

She inspected the dark green cover once more and then opened it up carefully. The old card spine crackled with the effort. Nicks flipped past the first page, which was lightly mottled and felt dry and delicate, like butterfly wings between her fingers. It was the first and only page she would turn. Her eyes settled on the second page and rapidly scanned left to right, left to right.

"What is it?" bleated an impatient Coral, who did not like to miss out.

"It's an inscription," murmured Nicks breathlessly. And then she read it out loud.

"*For my very best friend Coral, I have settled into our new family home, which still seems so far away. I miss you more than I can say – so perhaps this little book of poetry will make a better job of it. I hope to see you again, one day, soon. With my love always, your very best friend Betty.*"

So Betty *had* moved away from Sunday Harbour with her family. Nicks glanced up from the mottled page to her own very best friend standing right across from her. *History had come so close to repeating itself.* And then she smiled with relief.

Dipping her hand back inside the keepsakes box, she carefully unfolded the pink tissue protecting the two silver heart-shaped pendants they had found buried in the sand beneath the hut. "I think that we should wear these friendship necklaces," she finally said, slowly and carefully, like it meant something.

Nicks didn't need to give any reasons, of course Coral understood. Wearing the friendship necklaces would mean so much.

"It's like we're finally reuniting the girls," she said with a gentle smile. She knew that her great-aunt and Betty would have liked that very much.

Nicks rubbed her thumb across the silver heart engraved with the letter C before passing it over to her best friend. "We'll wear the lockets in memory of our great-aunts."

"And their friendship," added Coral as she fastened the clasp of the silver chain around her neck. It felt cold and heavy against her skin, but it soon warmed up. She stroked the pendant thoughtfully. It felt reassuring to know that it had once dangled from her great-aunt's neck. With the necklaces on, Coral and Nicks were no longer simply bound by the present – they were joined by their pasts too. And in a strange way, they had brought a bit of Great-Aunt Coral and Great-Aunt Betty back to life again. They would be best friends forever.